TEN-ACRE
ROCK

BOOKS BY KRIS LACKEY

THE BILL MAYTUBBY AND HANNAH BOND MYSTERIES

Nail's Crossing
Greasy Bend
Butcher Pen Road

A **BILL MAYTUBBY**
& **HANNAH BOND** MYSTERY

TEN-ACRE
ROCK

KRIS
A NOVEL
LACKEY

USA TODAY BESTSELLING AUTHOR

**BLACK
STONE**
PUBLISHING

First edition: 2023
ISBN 978-1-9826-8930-8
Fiction / Mystery & Detective / Police Procedural

Version 1

829 1102

Blackstone Publishing
31 Mistletoe Rd.
Ashland, OR 97520

www.BlackstonePublishing.com

For D.M.H.

CHAPTER 1

"What are we having for lunch today, Officer, uh . . ." The waiter glanced at Bill Maytubby's name tag. Then he shook his head and rolled his eyes up. "What am I talking about? Sergeant Maytubby. Sorry." He raised his pad of guest checks. "Tortilla soup. Cup, not bowl. No chips?" He squinted.

Maytubby smiled. "You got it." As the waiter scribbled, Maytubby touched his forearm gently. "If you could hold the order just a minute. I'm waiting for a friend." He didn't call the waiter by name.

The waiter stopped writing and pointed to a second Gonzalez Restaurant menu on the table, an ice water next to it. "I'm blind, too." He took Maytubby's menu. "To drink?"

"Water is good."

The waiter turned to go and then about-faced. "Is it the woman deputy"—he slide-whistled up, raised a flattened palm far above his head, and looked up at his hand—"Bond?"

"Yes, it is," Maytubby said.

The waiter slid the second menu off the table and again scratched on his pad. "Hannah always orders brisket tacos and extra guac and sour cream for lunch, a grande beef burrito if it's supper. Sweet tea." He smiled and turned toward the kitchen pass-through.

Maytubby looked out over the Tishomingo, Oklahoma, town square, commanded by the stately former capitol of the Chickasaw Nation. It was built before Oklahoma statehood, of local Pennington granite. Its silver cupola reflected the autumn sun. The nation's seat had decades ago removed to Ada, forty miles north.

Maytubby watched Deputy Bond's Johnston County patrol car turn left from Kemp Avenue and roll to a stop beside his Chickasaw Lighthorse Police cruiser. She swung open the door and set her left palm on the car's roof to heft her six feet and two inches into the daylight. Before shutting the door, she stood still and cast a cold eye over the town.

Maytubby had known Hannah since they trained together at the academy. He had pegged her as a rube, lumbering and silent. As the weeks passed, she outwitted their instructors and outshot her academy mates. Sometimes, near the end, she would look over at him when an instructor said something stupid. Her poker face killed him.

A punishing childhood had made her hard as a bois d'arc stump.

Now she walked slowly into the restaurant, appraising all the diners in the place as she walked directly to Maytubby's table without looking at it.

She must have spotted him through the restaurant window when she was well up the block.

Bond's duty belt creaked as she bent herself into a chair. She lowered the volume on her shoulder mike.

"Ruperto said he knew what you wanted."

Hannah nodded once. "I s'pose you ordered lettuce."

"Soup," Maytubby said.

"Either one nothin' but water." Hannah shook her head. "Water to eat and water to drink."

"I am nourished by righteousness," Maytubby said.

Hannah set her poker face and waited a beat. "I remember down on the Washita last winter you were nourished by a couple Slim Jims."

Maytubby smiled. "Touché." He drank some water. "Speaking of desperadoes on the Washita, I've been at the Golden Play casino all morning."

Hannah frowned. Maytubby's electrician friend Tom Hewitt had been shot dead behind the casino by a gang of arms traffickers who robbed an armored car. Maytubby and Bond tracked them and dealt rough justice on the Washita's muddy banks.

"I *thought* you smelled like cigarettes," she said.

"I went down there to arrest a criminal mastermind."

"Oh, didja, now," Hannah said. She spread her large hands on the table.

"Security detail carts money from the machines into a room where machines count it and sort it by denomination before it goes into zippered bags that are taken to a vault."

"Bags," Hannah said. "Let. Me. Guess." She rubbed an index finger on her cheek. "Some gomer took out his pocketknife and slit a hole in one of them bags so the dough would fall out."

Maytubby looked around the room and then back at Hannah. "All right. Steal my thunder."

"I was just thinkin' like a Carter County evil mastermind."

"There's a camera for every three square feet of the money route. Machines to counting room to vault to armored car. Everett Briggs, the head of security, howled when he showed me the tape of the guy crouching to pick up his loot."

Hannah blinked and patted the table with her right hand. "So you had to take the gomer to lockup in Pontotoc County."

"Yes."

"You been meltin' the asphalt this morning, Bill."

Ruperto appeared with a full serving tray in one hand and a folding tray stand in the other. He snapped open the stand and settled the tray on it.

When he had finished serving and folding the table, he looked at Hannah, rolled his eyes toward Maytubby's little cup of soup, and stage-whispered to Hannah, "Deputy, I would guard your food."

She looked at Ruperto and said, "He does it to himself."

Hannah emptied the ramekins of guacamole and sour cream over her tacos, then buried her teeth in the first one.

Maytubby still had a spoonful of soup in the bottom of his cup when Hannah finished her tacos, wiped her lips with her napkin, and laid it back on the table. Her cell phone buzzed in her pants pocket. She looked at her screen and then at Maytubby. "LeeRoy Sickles," she said.

"LeeRoy Sickles has a cell phone?" Maytubby said. He did not say, "And he's in your contacts?"

"Bond," she said. Then she held her phone to her ear while Maytubby finished his soup.

Sickles was a thin old baldpate who lived in a Territorial ruin at the end of Butcher Pen Road, near the defunct Bromide spas, their 1920s heyday long forgotten. Wielding an ancient 10-gauge shotgun, he had acted on intuition and rescued Maytubby from two yokel racketeers in their Bromide den.

A busboy arrived and began collecting their dishes.

"I know where it is," Bond said. "Which side of it?" She paused, then nodded. "You're sure it's a *dead* body."

The busboy froze for a second, said "Whoa!" under his breath, then finished and padded away.

"Yeah," Hannah said. "He's right here. I will. Be about ten minutes." She touched the phone and slid it back into her pocket. "LeeRoy says hidey."

Maytubby nodded once and looked at her.

"What?" she said.

"Nothin'." He faked a smirk.

"Shit. All right, then. I'm not tellin' you what exactly he found. It's on your way back to Ada, too."

Ruperto left the checks on the table and scurried off.

"You already did. He found a dead body," Maytubby said. He took a bill from his wallet and pinned it to the table with the saltshaker.

Hannah pulled some bills from her duty belt and tossed them on the table. "That's nothin'."

Maytubby said, "All right. I'll bite."

"You never heard this from me. I'm not telling Sheriff Magaw just yet." Hannah turned her head to make sure the table behind them was empty. "He found a skull in a charcoal kiln up by Ten-Acre Rock."

Maytubby tucked his chin. "Good thing I bit."

Bond leaned toward him. "LeeRoy says he thinks it's Indian land."

"Huh. I wonder why."

They rose together and walked out of the restaurant. When they were standing by their cruisers, Maytubby said, "That's ten miles from his house."

"Squirrel huntin', he says."

"Not with that cannon of his," Maytubby said.

Hannah shrugged, "Can't miss."

"Vapor of squirrel."

CHAPTER 2

Maytubby followed Bond's cruiser across the Rock Prairie, a boulder-strewn country of silica quarries and cattle ranches locally known as the Big Rock. Bond turned off the state highway onto Ten-Acre Rock Road. It twisted down to low-water crossings and up again into thickets of blackjack oak. Mica sparkled in the road's crushed granite.

Ten-Acre Rock sat massed above native grass and red cedars. Beyond it, the road wound into denser wood. Hannah's brake lights flashed, and she turned onto a rutted track. Crimson sumac bushes screeched against the cruiser's panels.

A once-beige Studebaker pickup was parked in front of a boulder at the trail's end. Maytubby pegged it as a sixties-era Champ. The cab was empty. Bond and Maytubby parked and walked on either side of the truck, then joined to walk slowly around the rock. They scanned the grassy patch between them and the trees, then stopped when they heard rustling. "Ooooooh"—a voice like a child's Halloween ghost. The footfalls approached, and the voice said "Goddamn!" just before a wiry bald man in a T-shirt and overalls ducked out of the blackjacks and into the sunlight. He jounced like a marionette, head twitching. LeeRoy Sickles cradled his mammoth 10-gauge double-barrel, its stock duct-taped and its swan-necked hammers uncocked. The barrel danced like a baton.

When he neared Bond and Maytubby, he halted and spun around. A russet mane flared and fell between his legs. Sickles grinned over his shoulder. "How you like my tail, Tall Drink?" He giggled. It was a stringer of dead squirrels he had tied to the back of his overalls.

When he turned around, Hannah said, "They're all tore up, LeeRoy."

Maytubby lowered his head and smiled when she used his first name.

LeeRoy's grin faded below his big black glasses. His body stilled. "I was hopin' you could fry 'em for your supper."

"You want me to break my teeth on bird shot?"

LeeRoy looked stricken. "You can chew soft and spit out the shot when you come to 'em."

Maytubby took in the rare sight of Hannah Bond softening. She was quiet for a few seconds. Then she said, "Sure. Let's get 'em in my trunk."

Sickles came back to life. As he jigged toward the cruiser, he lowered his head, reached over his left shoulder, and untied the stringer. Hannah opened the trunk, and he flopped the squirrels on the spare.

When they rejoined Maytubby, Sickles led them into the woods the way he had come. He carried the shotgun muzzle-down, on the crook of his right arm.

"How far is it?" Hannah said.

Sickles hunched and quivered. He spoke under his left armpit. "Why? You playin' hooky, Tall Drink?" He looked forward and giggled.

"Still on my lunch break. I eat fast."

Sickles held a low limb until Bond grabbed it and held it for Maytubby.

Maytubby said, "I don't see a fence."

"Ain't airn fence on this side of the land. Never was. I been huntin' up here forever."

Maytubby looked down at the first fallen leaves. "Why do you think this is Indian land?"

Sickles may have shrugged. It was hard to tell. He bent his head back and shouted, "Heard it! Lot o' times!" He stopped suddenly and faced his companions. He threw his torso back and flattened his palms on his kidneys, as if he were in pain. "Only building on this whole section is a tar-paper shack halfway to Ten-Acre Rock."

Sickles fished a pack of cigarettes out of his top overall pocket, shook it, and lipped one out. He pinched a matchbook out of the cellophane, lit the cigarette, shook the match out. After he replaced the pack, he raised his cigarette hand over his head, made a tripod of his free fingers, and planted them on his bald pate.

"Weirdo couple has lived in it a coon's age. They got chickens and a couple hogs, drive a cockeyed motorcycle into different little towns to get groceries and Coleman fuel—I guess, for a lantern. Got a woodpile for cookin' and heat. Must haul water from somewheres. Might have a pump. Nobody seems to know their names." The ash on his cigarette grew long and fell on his head. "And after some people got too close to the shed and seen a gun barrel poke out the front door, they didn't go 'round there no more. Whoever those folks are, they don't make trouble in the towns, so the law leaves 'em alone. You know 'em, Tall Drink?"

Hannah shook her head.

Sickles brought the cigarette to his mouth and inhaled deeply. Then he flicked the butt on the forest floor and exhaled a plume of blue smoke. Maytubby waited for Sickles to turn and walk on before he ground out the butt with his heel.

Fifteen minutes later, Sickles led them to the edge of a small clearing and stopped. His body stilled. Bond and Maytubby broke single file and stood on his right and left. In the shade just beyond the clearing was what looked like a short wall of planks, about ten feet long, with dirt mounded behind it. New stovepipe rose from one end. Maytubby's *inko'si'*, his uncle, had made a charcoal kiln, so he knew that there was a twin plank wall on the other side to brace the dirt. The mound would cover several fifty-five-gallon drums, lying on their sides and welded together, an intake port for both air and combustion wood were cut out of the barrel top opposite the stovepipe. Two large hinged doors, cut from the barrel nearest the stovepipe, made way for the wood meant to be turned to charcoal. The doors would then be buried under the dirt.

A few feet to the left of the stovepipe was a makeshift forge in an old wringer washing machine, connected by PVC pipe to a homemade box bellows.

Maytubby said, "Where is the body, Mr. Sickles?"

"In the business end, where they cook charcoal."

"LeeRoy, I think the sergeant is about to take pictures of our boot soles."

Sickles scratched his head and reached for his cigarettes. "Good sense," he said, and paused. "Unless one of us done it." He grinned and wrinkled his nose.

"If you could wait on the smoke until you get back to your vehicle?" Maytubby said.

Sickles stared at the pack a second, then half closed his eyes, like a drunk person. "They *would* think I done it, then." He slid the pack back into his overalls pocket. "But I had a couple when I was huntin'."

Maytubby thumbed his phone to the camera and took a step back. Bond stepped back as well, crossed her right leg over her left, and tilted her sole toward the camera. When she lowered her foot, Maytubby said, "You're six two, so that's about a size twelve?"

"Yeah," she said. "Extra wide."

Maytubby typed in a caption and photographed his own sole.

Sickles shifted his gun and set its stock on the ground. He grasped the barrel for balance and imitated the others by standing on one leg and crossing the other. Maytubby photographed his boot sole, which was worn almost flat, and the print of the shotgun's butt. "You done?" Sickles said.

"Yeah. You know your shoe size?" Maytubby said.

Sickles took up his shotgun and blew a raspberry. "D'I look like a man who'd know that? I buy all my shoes and clothes at farm auctions. Dead men's clothes, dollar a box. I wear what fits and burn the rest in the trash barrel."

Maytubby nodded and typed in "Size 9." He asked Sickles where he had walked to look inside the kiln.

Sickles raised his left arm and described circles in the air. "Oh, hell, I walked all over. I ain't seen a charcoal kiln since I's a kid. I was curious. Then I seen the dirt had been clawed away from the hatches. I expected because they wanted to get at the finished charcoal. But when I opened the hatch, well, you'll see."

"Lead on," Hannah said.

She and Maytubby followed Sickles single file to limit the footprints. When they arrived at the kiln, they stood side by side. Bond snapped open a pouch on her duty belt and pulled out a latex glove. She grabbed the handle of the door nearest the flue. When she pulled it back, the hinges squealed.

Snaggled yellow incisors, one chipped, grimaced from a blackened human skull. Other bones lay helter-skelter beneath it. To the right of the skull, a brown plastic glob with grayish bands around it sprouted singed fabric.

"Chuck Taylor," Maytubby said.

Sickles turned bug eyes on him. "You *know* this mess?"

"Line of high-top sneakers made by Converse. Plastic blob is the right color for a sole."

"You gonna take a picture of that, too, Sergeant?" Sickles said. "He might of got sick and tard of life and taken a runnin' jump in there." His shoulders danced merrily. The shotgun barrel knocked against the shoring planks.

Bond and Maytubby ignored the remark. Maytubby pulled out his phone and photographed the skull and blob in case kiln robbers should visit the site. He also dropped a pin in Google Maps and sent it to himself so he could pass it along.

"Hee hee hee! He *done* it!" Sickles said.

When Maytubby had replaced his phone, he said, "The sole binding, on the outside, used to be white—those little bands around the blob. And the fabric's likely canvas. The OSBI techs are going to find metal eyelets in the ashes. Ventilation holes."

Hannah closed the door and peeled off her glove. She also photographed the scene with her phone. She turned to LeeRoy. "Lead on. I don't want that artillery anywhere I can't see it."

Again his body twitched and lurched. Hannah, who walked just behind him, said, "So that's the first you've seen of that kiln?"

"Yes'm. Wasn't nothin' there, end of last winter."

Hannah said, "You think the hermits in the tar-paper shack built it?"

Sickles made some glottal noises as he went along. Then he said, "Makin' charcoal for a forge is a thing they might do. Make 'em some hog-butcherin' tools. Like a gambrel." With his free hand, he scratched his head furiously. "On the other hand, how did they cut and weld those barrels? Don't seem like they'd have gear like that. Also, there was a shitload of tire tracks in front of that boulder when I come this mornin'. Might be other folks. Yahoos all over this country."

When they rounded the boulder, Maytubby asked Sickles and Bond to wait while he photographed and captioned the tire treads on all three vehicles. The Studebaker had four different tires. Then he bent and photographed every tread print he could see at the end of the trail. He also photographed the Studebaker.

Hannah said, "We appreciate you telling us about this, LeeRoy. We're going to notify the sheriff and the Oklahoma Bureau of Investigation and hang some crime tape around the scene."

Sickles nodded rapidly while he laid the 10 gauge in the Studebaker's bed.

"Hey, LeeRoy," Hannah said.

Sickles turned toward her, lowered his chin, and peered over his black-framed glasses. "Yeah, Tall Drink?"

"Some state cops will be coming to your house to ask you questions."

Sickles threw his head back and reached for the pack of smokes in his overalls pocket. "Ooooooh. Goddamn. I figured."

"Do us a favor and don't wave that gun at 'em."

He opened the pickup door, hopped into the cab, and lit a filter-less cigarette. He grinned at Bond through the open window. "Okay." He took a long drag and exhaled. He looked at her. "Would be fun to skeer 'em, though." His shoulders danced as he started the truck and clutched it into reverse.

CHAPTER 3

Bond and Maytubby watched the Studebaker part the sea of red sumac and disappear. As Bond pulled out her phone, she said, "That's a lot of letters to put on a tailgate."

Bond said, "You want the sheriff to call your Lighthorse Police chief after he calls OSBI, or you want to admit you been loitering here with me and LeeRoy?"

"I'll call Chief Fox myself. Honesty is the best policy," Maytubby said.

Bond gave him the side-eye. "When there's nothin' to lose."

"I'll send my pics and the Google pin to Sheriff Magaw so OSBI and the medical examiner can find the spot." Maytubby scratched his chin with his phone. "FBI? If this is Indian Country and if perp or victim is a tribal member."

She nodded. "I'll remind Magaw."

They walked apart as they called their bosses. A lone turkey buzzard wheeled in the sky.

Bond finished first. She opened the trunk of her cruiser, yanked out a roll of crime scene tape from under the dead squirrels, and shut the lid. When Maytubby had pocketed his phone, he stood behind the Lighthorse cruiser. "You think we need two?"

"Be faster," she said.

Maytubby found his tape and joined her on the path. They walked briskly and said nothing. Blackjack acorns snapped under their boots. When they reached the clearing edge, Bond started with a red cedar trunk on the left, Maytubby with a hackberry trunk on his right. They separated, worked fast, and met twenty yards behind the kiln.

As they were tying up their ends, Bond's shoulder radio crackled. They stood up and looked at it.

"Bond," she said.

"Hannah," the dispatcher said, "single-vehicle accident with injury reported on State Seven between Indian Church and Saw Mill. Ambulance and trooper on the way."

Bond was already hustling down the path when she said, "I'm three miles out. Tell the sheriff to send Eph to watch this crime scene till OSBI gets here." Then she leaned into a sprint, the tape roll slapping greasegrass. Maytubby had to lay down more steps to keep up.

———————

As Bond turned east on Oklahoma 7, Maytubby following her, she could see up ahead a pickup stopped on each shoulder of the pavement, and the rear of a Highway Patrol cruiser with flashing overheads in the center of the highway. Before she reached the cruiser, it sped away. "Huh," Bond said.

When she had pulled onto the shoulder behind one truck and Maytubby had eased in front of the other, they turned on their strobes and walked onto the road. The pickup drivers were climbing into their cabs.

Bond saw the Studebaker in the bar ditch before she saw the rear end of Sickles's overalls sticking out of the Johnsongrass just below the highway grade. She strode toward him. Behind her, Maytubby stepped down into the weeds and moved to the Studebaker.

The pickups pulled onto the highway and drove away.

Just before Bond reached Sickles, he stood up and turned

toward her. Blood glistened on his face and soaked his T-shirt and the tops of his overalls. His glasses were missing, and his eyes looked very small.

"That you, Big Sister?" he said, spreading his arms for balance. Maytubby came up behind him and grabbed a hank of denim in each fist to hold the old man steady.

"It's me. Wh—"

"That trooper seen you comin' and took out after the sons a bitches I told him run me off the road." He reached under Maytubby's arm, yanked a red bandanna from his overalls hip pocket, and wiped blood off his forehead and mouth. "Help me find my specs." He spat in the weeds.

"Okay," Hannah said. "You think they're in the truck?"

"Oooooh, goddamn." He flicked the bandanna at the sky. "Who knows."

Bond searched in the weeds as she trudged toward the truck. She pulled open the heavy steel door with ease and let it fall on the back of her thighs as she leaned into the cab and probed under the seat. The glasses were wedged in a cushion spring. She pried them loose and saw that one of the lenses was cracked.

She walked halfway up the ditch bank and stood in front of LeeRoy. He said, "You got 'em?"

She unfolded the earpieces and slid the glasses onto his face. "They're a little broke," she said.

Sickles opened his eyes wide and nodded. "Not my shootin' eye, at least." Blood from a gash in his forehead pooled on the lower rims of his glasses. He crunched the bandanna and pressed it against the cut. "Speakin' of, where's my gun at?"

"I'll find it," Bond said. She waded through the Johnsongrass and found it between the Studebaker and the fence line. She broke the shotgun at the breech and pulled out the two shells. "Got it," she called. "I'll put it back in the bed. Shells in your glove box."

"You can let go, Sergeant Chickasaw. I can walk good." He paused a second. "I think." Maytubby obeyed but held his hand against

Sickles's back until the old man turned around. Bond joined them. "Look where they hit me," he said, pointing at the pickup's left rear side panel. There was a small crease with a smear of black paint above it. "Black GMC. I thought he was passin' me. Then he slowed down. Jerked over and hit me. Couldn't see who was inside."

An ambulance approached from the east. Siren off, strobes lit.

Bond said, "The trooper see it happen?"

Sickles shook the bandanna out, balled it up again, and held it against the wound with his left hand. He spat twice on his bloody right hand and wiped it on the bib of his overalls. "No, but he was here right quick. Helped me out of the truck. I told him about the GMC. He said as soon as help came he would chase after the Beezlebub."

When the ambulance stopped on the asphalt, Sickles, Maytubby, and Bond turned and watched two beefy male EMTs clamber out and glove up.

"Oooooh, goddamn," Sickles said. "I ain't goin'. Tell 'em, big sister."

Maytubby's cell buzzed. He answered it as he walked toward his cruiser.

To Sickles, Hannah said, "You might of broke your skull, LeeRoy. You got Medicare, right?"

The EMTs edged toward them and stopped.

Sickles said, "Ain't that I fear. It's what comes tied to its tail."

Hannah nodded and said to the EMTs, "He's refusing the ambulance, guys. You got some butterfly bandages for his head?"

One said, "I got it," and turned away.

The other smiled at Sickles and walked slowly toward him. "Mr. . . ?"

"Poontang," LeeRoy said. He raised his shoulders and stuck out his chin.

Hannah snorted and looked away.

"Oh," the EMT said. "Sir, can you see up close okay without your glasses?"

"Why?" LeeRoy said.

"Take off your specs," Hannah said. "He wants to see if you got a concussion."

LeeRoy pulled them off and folded them gingerly.

The EMT stood before him and moved his index finger in front of his nose. "Keep your head still and watch my finger," the EMT said. He slowly moved his finger up and down, left and right. "That looks good," he said. "Now look all around and tell me if you have . . . if you're seeing double."

LeeRoy rolled his eyes around and shrugged. "No."

"Can you tell me how you got that cut?"

LeeRoy's nostrils flared. "Some peckerwood run me into the bar ditch!"

The EMT nodded. His companion arrived and said, "Okay?"

"Patch 'im up, bro."

As LeeRoy's head was being swabbed and bandaged, Hannah saw Maytubby walking toward her. She set her hands on her duty belt and said, "Thanks, guys." To Maytubby she said, "Renaldo was our trooper, I guess."

"He was. Jake sighted what he thinks was the GMC on Three-Seventy-Seven northbound. It accelerated when he got within a hundred yards—too far to get a tag number. He hit the overheads, and the truck kicked it up, spun onto Spring Creek Road at Connerville, and stairstepped back west. It just beat a train on the Samson quarry siding, and Jake got cut off by a gang of hopper cars."

"I'm hearin' that!" Sickles said. The EMT had just planted the last butterfly. LeeRoy swatted his arm away and scowled. He bent at the waist and kicked a stone over the fence.

The EMT wadded his trash, joined his partner in the cab. Hannah could hear them laughing as they drove away. Sickles turned a baleful face toward the ambulance.

Hannah let him stew a minute. Then she said, "LeeRoy!" His head snapped around. "I'll call Garn to tow you out of the ditch. Follow me down to my place. We can skin these squirrels. I'll flour 'em and fry us dinner. Make some gravy."

"I can't afford no wrecker, Big Sister."

"It's okay. I owe Garn a favor. Besides, I need a minute to write up the incident."

Sickles pulled his pack of cigarettes out of his overalls, shook one out, lit it. "Why's he gonna do that if you owe *him* a favor?"

Bond slid her cell from her pants pocket. "That's how humans think. They like you to owe 'em."

While she was waiting for Garn to answer, Maytubby walked to her, touched her shoulder, and pointed west. She nodded, and he walked back to his cruiser.

Sickles leaned his head back, inhaled a lungful of smoke, held it a few seconds, and exhaled through his nose. "Damn if you ain't right."

CHAPTER 4

Maytubby made a U-turn and headed back west. After he passed Indian Church Road, sedans from the Oklahoma medical examiner and OSBI passed in the opposite direction. After he turned north on State 1, he passed a wide field of towering white wind turbines. Most were still under construction, their massive blades frozen against the sky.

A few minutes later, quarry conveyor towers loomed in the yellowing light. He turned west onto Samson Road, which struck the siding crossing where Renaldo had lost the GMC. Pickups driven by quarry workers coming off shift thumped over the rails, going home to Mill Creek and Tishomingo. Maytubby crept past them. There were two black GMCs, but any damage would be on the opposite side. He passed a yard jammed with idle hopper cars.

The dirt road skirted tailing heaps and electric-blue ponds. Bullet-riddled OPEN PIT signs dangled from rusted gates. When he had passed the quarry, he stopped and took a pair of field glasses out of the glove box. At each ranch gate, he slowed and glassed the modest house at the end of a long dirt driveway. Now and then a pickup from the quarry roared around him, veiling the cruiser in sand. He stair-stepped on the gridded roads because there was no bridge over Mill

Creek. He reached State 7 without seeing another black GMC. The truck that hit LeeRoy might be in Sulphur—or Dallas, for that matter. He turned toward Lighthorse Police headquarters in Ada.

Just beyond Scullin, his phone buzzed. "What are you doing?" his fiancée, Jill Milton, said.

"Foraging, like any man worth his salt."

"Anything for dinner?" Jill said.

"Oh, yeah. A peck of bur oak acorns. The ones big as apri—"

"I know what they look like, buster. What are we supposed to do with them?" she said.

"According to ethnobotanists who are wise in the customs of our ancestors, roast them in coals."

"In that case, I better gather kindling and make a fire in the yard."

"That's what I would do," Maytubby said.

"You're full of prunes. Are you coming over?"

A whitetail buck bounded over a cattle fence onto the highway. Maytubby stomped his brakes and dropped the cell. The deer jumped the opposite fence and bounded away. Maytubby pulled to the shoulder, stopped, and retrieved the phone from the floorboard.

"What was that?" Jill said.

"Buck on the road."

"Oh, yeah. It's rut."

"Which means yes, I'll be over. Soon as I get my truck and don my stalking garb."

"The camo dozer cap and goober teeth," Jill said. Maytubby heard NPR news in the background.

"How well you have learned the nuances of deep cover."

"How well I have learned that when the goober teeth appear, you're going to leave without honoring your duties as a lover."

Maytubby noticed a black pickup in his rearview. A quarter mile back. Not gaining on him. "My intrepid nocturnal forays don't whet your lust?"

"Could you bring an onion?"

"Roger that."

She raspberried before she hung up.

The black pickup stayed behind him to the Ada city limits. It turned onto a bypass just before he reached the headquarters of the Chickasaw Lighthorse Police. He took his field glasses out of the cruiser's glove box and tossed them through the open passenger window of his pickup.

In the Plexiglas HQ intake foyer, Maytubby had raised his hand to type in the entry code when the dispatcher, Sheila, buzzed him in. "Hey, Pilgrim," she said.

"Hey, Sheila." He let the "Pilgrim" alone.

"I heard about the skull in the kiln. You got summons receipts?"

Maytubby pulled them from his shirt pocket and handed them to her.

"Chief Fox wants to see you," she said.

Maytubby watched her unfold the paperwork and smooth it with her palm. Her straightened fingers reminded him of something she had once told him: in her days with other law enforcement agencies, she had taken up smoking so she could burn the arms of staff who tried to grope her.

"Thanks, Sheila."

He walked through two dim hallways to his boss's glass-enclosed office. Before he knocked, he watched Fox at his computer, its blue screen reflected in his glasses. On the wall behind him, the nation's governor smiled down from a large framed photograph. Maytubby knocked. He noticed the screen color change in Fox's glasses before the chief waved him in. Maytubby knew his boss watched bass-fishing channels on YouTube.

Fox swiveled to face Maytubby and leaned back in his chair. "This LeeRoy . . . What is it, Stickles?"

"Sickles. Like hammer and."

Fox blinked and shook his head. Then he brightened. "We gonna have to put him on the payroll?" Fox smiled.

"First, better see if he fires that howitzer at the agent coming down Butcher Pen Road tomorrow."

Fox plucked a rubber band from his desk, looped it over his thumbs, and stretched it. "Sheriff Magaw said he talked with OSBI. They got a team at the site."

"Magaw talk with Scrooby?"

"Oh, yeah. Your old friend." Fox grinned. "Listen." He shot the rubber band at the computer screen and leaned forward in his chair. "I'll contact the nation tomorrow and see if the crime scene really is tribal land. I doubt it. But you know, with that McGirt decision by the Supreme Court, if we had an anglo perp and an Indian victim, the US Attorney would be prosecuting—not the state—if the crime was committed anywhere in the original Chickasaw Nation."

Maytubby nodded. "Not just on our little remnant of tribal land."

"Right. The feds and us are like those guys at the Alamo. Gonna need a lot more men."

"Or women," Maytubby said. "More women than men getting law degrees now."

"Yeah, yeah." Fox waved his hand dismissively. Then he stood. "Listen. Murray County is holding a pickpocket caught in the Sulphur casino. I need you to bring him home to Pontotoc lockup in the morning." Fox slid an envelope from under the corner of his keyboard and handed it to Maytubby. "You'll see the prisoner's name is Cross." Fox sat down and swiveled to face his screen.

As Maytubby shut the door, he wondered whether Fox was giving him make-work to keep him off the murder or giving him make-work close to the crime scene so he could meddle off the books.

He walked past his own office door without a glance, waved goodbye to Sheila, and walked out to his white-over-bronze 1965 Ford pickup. Its T. rex V-8 roared to life, and he edged onto Ada's Main Street in quest of an onion.

CHAPTER 5

Hannah Bond still wore her deputy uniform when she tilted LeeRoy's plate of squirrel bones onto her own. A haze of bacon grease and Lee-Roy's cigarette smoke hung over her austere kitchen.

The bones and smell removed her to her foster father's hovel, where he had raped and killed her little sister. Way to hell and gone in the San Bois Mountains, long ago. In those days, she waited until the old man was drunk, then took to the woods with his single-shot .22 rifle to put food on the bench he called a table.

When she had driven Sickles home in her old Buick Skylark, she kept an eye on the rearview. At the edge of Tish, on her way home, a black GMC pickup passed her, heading the way she had come. Oklahoma plate.

She picked up a tiny drumstick and sucked it clean, then dumped the bones and LeeRoy's cigarette butts into the trash, drew some water in the sink, and dunked the dishes to soak. She would scour the iron skillet with salt later. She heated old coffee in a pan and poured it into a thermos, tossed some venison jerky in a paper bag.

She hung her uniform over a chair and put on jeans, a checkered flannel shirt, and a black canvas hoodie. Her duty belt lay on her bed, alongside her barbell-size Steiner binoculars, which she had brought from the cruiser. She removed her old Smith and Wesson Model 10 and stuck it in the back of her jeans. Her ID and Maglite went into her jacket pocket. The Steiners she would have to carry.

At dusk, Bond again wound up Butcher Pen Road toward Sickles's unpainted Territorial house. She crept past a crude stone replica of Roman Jerusalem. It was half-finished, abandoned by its yokel builders—the Medicare fraudsters LeeRoy had helped Maytubby and Bond run to ground. The warped hand-lettered sign advertising THE HOLEY CITY COMMING SOON for throngs of future tourists was still there. Someone had painted "ASS-" above "HOLEY." LeeRoy, Bond assumed.

In failing light, she switched off her headlights and made her way to a stand of post oaks where the bar ditch was shallow. She backed under the canopy. Here she could keep an eye on the road and LeeRoy's house. The old man's glasses were broken; he would shit fire if he saw her here.

She cranked her window all the way down.

––––––––––––––

An acorn smacking the Skylark's roof woke her—a little after eleven, by her watch. She yawned and drank coffee from the mouth of the thermos, gnawed a hunk of jerky.

Sickles's house was dark. Coyotes yelped in the hills above Bromide. A waning hunter's moon cast the land in cold blue.

Just before two, Bond heard a low engine sound and gravel popping. She leaned over the bench seat, rolled down the passenger window, grasped the massive Steiners, and raised them from the seat. Far down Butcher Pen Road, she saw a dark pickup, its headlights dark, moonlight reflected in its windshield.

She threw down the binoculars, snugged the dark hood over her head, and opened the car door. The dome bulb had burned out years ago. She closed the door quietly and loped into the bar ditch. Moonlight guided her along the roadside ditch as she picked up her pace toward LeeRoy's house. Its steep, rusted tin roof took out a chunk of sky.

Bond remembered a knot of chokecherry bushes hugging the front porch. She coaxed the revolver out of her jeans and moved the Maglite to the kangaroo pocket in her hoodie. The pickup crept into view at the end of Sickles's long sand driveway, a hundred yards away.

Halfway up the drive, the pickup's brake lights briefly flashed red on the brush behind it. Then the engine fell silent. The driver's door opened. The dome light silhouetted two forms: a short figure in the passenger seat, and a tall thick form bundling out of the cab with a thin dark object, probably a rifle, in one hand, and a shorter one in the other. The dome light went dark. Bond watched the moonlit man stoop and walk very slowly. His face was almost white in the moonlight. Whiter than a human face, Bond thought. Black pantyhose work a lot better than a mask like that.

The man stopped and stood upright, his arms weighted straight down. The white mask turned from side to side. Then he turned his head toward Butcher Pen Road for a few seconds before setting it back toward the house. Now he crouched again and padded with real haste directly toward Bond. She aimed her revolver, drew out the Maglite with her left hand and held it, still unlit, parallel to the barrel.

Up in the bur oak above Sickles's house, a screech owl unleashed its piercing infant scream. The man froze. Bond stood, aimed her pistol, and switched on her Maglite. The man wore a child's princess mask, with smiling red lips and a red bow in its plastic hair. He dropped whatever was in his left hand and brought that hand to the forestock of his long gun.

"Deputy!" Bond shouted. "Drop your weapon now! Now!"

The man pivoted and ran toward his pickup, a black GMC. Before Bond could give chase, a door burst open on LeeRoy's porch. She knew better than to get between the old man and his quarry. Sure enough, the instant the pickup's dome light blinked on, Sickles let fly with two volleys from his cannon.

Pinging metal and exploding glass, followed by the roar of the pickup's engine. Hannah figured Sickles had to reload. She sprinted toward the truck. It kicked into reverse and spun up a whirlwind of dust and pebbles. Bond kept running, shielding her eyes with the Maglite hand. The pickup's brake lights flashed an instant before it yawed. When it was crosswise in the drive, she lowered her light and, through the dust, caught a glimpse of front-end damage on the truck just before it shuddered forward toward Butcher Pen Road. Bond panted, running harder, jabbed her pistol into the hoodie pocket, and moved the Maglite into her gun hand. Not thirty yards from the tailgate when it began to recede, she trained her light on the license plate bracket as she slowed. Not only was the plate lamp out, there was no plate. But the beam caught a silver dealer decal on the gate.

"Shit!" she said as she ducked and ran perpendicular to the road. A second later, two more booms from LeeRoy's 10 gauge followed the pickup. Bond heard the *whow* of the bird shot, then its patter on the roadside leaves.

"It's Hannah! LeeRoy! Don't shoot! I'm comin' up!"

She caught her breath, moved her pistol to the back of her jeans as she walked toward the house. "You hear me, LeeRoy?"

"Come on!" he shouted.

Her hoodie's neck was soaked. The air smelled of gunpowder and exhaust. Sickles's porch light came on. When she mounted the steps, she saw that he was wearing women's cat-eye glasses. With rhinestones. His gun was broken at the breech, draped over his left forearm. Four spent shotgun shells lay on the porch around his bare feet. He still wore the overalls. The tics were gone; his body was at rest.

Bond stowed her flashlight and caught her breath.

"You think I need a babysitter, Big Sister?"

"Where'd you get those lady glasses?" Bond said.

"Think back," he said.

She nodded. "Oh, yeah. The farm auction boxes."

LeeRoy blinked. "Kinda tight, but you seen how good they work. With the broke ones I might of shot *you*."

"He wore a mask and had a long gun. I think a rifle."

"Is that what you were yellin' about?"

"Yup," Bond said. "And he dropped something in your yard."

Sickles laid his gun on the porch and stuck out his chin. "Well, hell, let's see what it was." He scampered down the stairs. Bond pulled out her flashlight and followed him.

"Got!" he spat, hopping on one foot. "Dern goathead." Bond shined the light on his foot until he got it out. Then she swept the yard with the flashlight as they walked.

"There." He pointed. "What the hell is that? A post driver?"

They stepped closer. She lit it up. "It's an entry ram. Two-foot. Cops use 'em to bust down doors."

"Hee hee hee," LeeRoy giggled. Now his body began to twitch, and he jiggled his cat eyes with his hand. "Sister, my door don't even have a latch. He would've swung that thing and come flyin' in there like a blind jackass."

Hannah snorted.

"Gored hisself on that old steer-horn hat rack. Hee hee hee."

She walked toward the house. "Looks like we spared his life."

"*And* perserved his dignity," LeeRoy cackled from behind.

When they had mounted the porch, Hannah mopped her face with her sleeve. "A state officer will be here tomorrow—"

"Ooooh, goddamn," LeeRoy grimaced.

"To ask you questions about finding the kiln. And probably about you shooting that truck. They will be in an unmarked white car. Don't shoot 'em. And don't touch that ram. Another agent may come to dust and photograph it." She pointed at the shells on the porch. "Leave those there, too. I'll tell the sheriff what happened, and he'll pass that along to the state folks."

LeeRoy stared at his feet and wiggled his toes. Then he raised his head and pushed the cat eyes up his nose. "Maybe I should bake a cake."

CHAPTER 6

Maytubby scored a Spanish onion at Dicus Market and drove three blocks to his gable-and-wing house, built when Ada was IT—Indian Territory. It perched on the bank of an old Katy railroad cut, now a paved bike path. Walking to his porch, he crunched acorns and fallen leaves.

To light his front room, he pushed a button. The house was wired in 1932 and never updated—a perennial code-dodger. Maytubby savored his house during Oklahoma's brief autumns. The late afternoon sun chiseled shadows on its wooden floors, and mild air drifted through its crannies. A sycamore off the porch sweetened the rooms.

In his bedroom he switched on a night-table lamp, which lit a worn edition of Emily Dickinson's poems. He hung up his uniform, laid his duty belt on the bed, and pulled on black jeans, a black T-shirt, and a ratty camo sweatshirt. From the closet shelf he took down a raggedy camo earflap cap and snugged it on his head.

He opened the top drawer of his dresser and plucked out an elastic Petzl headlamp and his trusty set of goober teeth. The Petzl he fitted on his cap; then the teeth went into his jeans pocket. In a pinch, he could ditch the Petzl, but the pair of black New Balance trail runners he laced up would be a city-boy giveaway. Cross that bridge later. He slung his duty belt over his shoulder and switched off the lamp.

In the kitchen, lit by a single bulb at the end of long braided wires, he opened his Eisenhower-era Frigidaire and removed a bag of shelled pecans and a Bosc pear. He filled a water bottle from the tap. On his way out, he pushed the Off buttons for kitchen and front room. The dangling porch light he left burning.

Before he opened the pickup door, he glanced at the bed—empty except for a spare tire chained to a stake pocket. If he left the truck on a country road, an empty bed would raise suspicion. He gathered a rake and hoe and shovel leaning against his house and laid them in the bed. Still not convincing. He flicked on the Petzl and walked to an old stone well he had covered with plywood. One of the former owners of his house was a drinker who had filled the well with empty pint bottles. Maytubby slid the plywood off the top, grabbed and cradled a half dozen bottles, and replaced the cover. He carried the bottles to his truck and scattered them over the bed. Their labels were long gone, but any hooch in a storm. On his way to Jill's apartment, he stopped at a liquor store on Mississippi Street and bought a half-pint of cheap whiskey in a plastic bottle. Before he got back in his pickup, he drained half of it on the parking lot asphalt and slid the bottle into his pants pocket.

A few minutes later, Maytubby drove between rock driveway pillars, past one of the 1920s oil-boom mansions on the crest of King's Road, to Jill Milton's garage apartment. Her great-grandfather, the son of a Chickasaw freedman, had lived in the same apartment when he chauffeured the oil upstart in the big house. A descendant of Africans enslaved by Chickasaws, he had married a woman who was half Chickasaw.

Still wearing the earflap cap, Maytubby stopped on the wobbly stairs to listen as Jill clawhammered the sawmill-minor tune "Cluck Old Hen" on her Deering banjo. The melancholy air fit the dying autumn light.

Jill was settling the banjo in its stand when Maytubby came inside. She was wearing an olive sweater with a cowl neckline, jeans, and black ankle boots.

She looked at the onion. "And you call yourself a forager."

He held out the onion with mock contrition.

"You'll get no quarter from me." She pointed to a chef's knife lying on the kitchen counter. "Mince!" She plugged her phone into speakers and swiped to Satie's *Sarabandes*.

Maytubby set the onion on a chopping board. Then he looked at some chicken thighs and drumsticks on a plate. "Wait," he said. "Is that Cluck Old Hen?"

"You heard the funeral dirge."

He took off his cap and held it over his heart.

"All right, all right," she said. "Get rid of that thing."

He hung the hat on a kitchen chair and washed his hands in the sink.

Jill said, "Rose, at the tribal demonstration kitchen, dispatched a few spent hens. She cleaned them and kept the breasts for her shows." She began chopping thyme and rosemary on another board.

Maytubby skinned the onion and took his knife to it. Tears began to roll down his cheeks. "Cluck was a good old hen." He sniffed. "She laid eggs for the railroad men."

Jill nodded. "Sometimes one, sometimes two."

"Just enough," Maytubby pretended to sob, "for the railroad crew."

Jill laughed and wiped her knife on the board's edge. She set the knife down and stepped to Maytubby's side. "I have persimmons from the yard," she whispered in his ear.

He ceased chopping. "Is it true they render women helpless to male advances?"

"We're about to find out." She squeezed his ass and bit his earlobe.

He laid his head on her shoulder and said, "Tell me, does Rose use persimmons in the demo kitchen?"

"Shut your mouth. The nation embraces Protestant Christianity." Jill lit her tiny oven with a kitchen match, shut the oven door, and canted the match to keep it alive. Then she lit a burner on the stove and blew the match out. She set a big iron skillet on the burner, drizzled olive oil in the bottom, waited a minute, and then added the chicken pieces, skin side down.

Jill had inherited two things from the freedman: the iron skillet and a 1915 Springfield shotgun. A year earlier, when Maytubby and Bond were in a firefight with members of a country crime ring down on the Washita, the gang's boss had come looking for Maytubby and broken down her door. She had seen him out her window, loaded the freedman's Springfield, and sent him to the Mercy Hospital ER.

She passed Maytubby the bowl with the persimmons. "Squeeze out the pulp and take out the seeds. Throw the skins and seeds away. The skins are indigestible. They make bezoars in your gut."

Maytubby took the bowl. "*Bed* sores? In your gut?"

"Buh-*zoars*. Like hairballs. Only they're stones. Specifically, phytobezoars. Persimmon skins have lots of tannin," she said.

"Thanks for telling me that. I've eaten persimmons since I was a kid."

"I could use a doorstop around here on windy days." Jill took a spatula and flipped the thighs. "Onion, sous chef."

Maytubby tilted his board and nudged the minced onion into the pan with his knife. Jill dropped in the persimmon pith and scattered half the chopped rosemary and thyme into the oil.

"'Sous chef.' I bet you learned that in your server days in Brooklyn. Probably from that fire-eater hipster. The dude from Texarkana."

Jill took a bottle of cold sauvignon blanc from her refrigerator. "As a matter of fact."

"You lie!" Maytubby took a corkscrew from the counter. Jill handed him the bottle.

"I knew other men at NYU."

Maytubby pulled the cork. He affected a playground sneer and wagged his head. "Well, I knew other women at St. John's." He took two wineglasses from the cabinet, set them on the counter, and poured the wine.

"Yeah, those daughters of Great Books hippies from Sheboygan." She took a glass and sipped it. "Not bad for the local winery. Pour some olive oil in a bowl and get me a whisk."

Maytubby drank a little wine, set the glass down, and complied. Jill walked to the end of the counter, opened a cabinet, stood on tiptoe, and brought down a bottle from the top shelf.

"What is that?" he said.

"Sorghum syrup," she said.

"What! The poison you have labored to banish from our diabetes-plagued nation?"

She poured a few tablespoons into the oil and tossed in the rest of the herbs. "It's a glaze, not a quart of grape soda." She capped the bottle and put it back on the shelf.

Maytubby whisked the syrup and oil, poured the mixture over the chicken. "Camel's nose under the tent." He opened the oven door, and Jill slid the skillet in.

"Discretion is the better part of valor," she said.

"The boring part." Maytubby lit the candles on her drop-leaf table and set out plates and utensils while Jill leaned against the counter and sipped her wine. Satie's quiet piano chords lingered. "Where did you stage the healthy-veggie roadshow today?" Maytubby took his wine and stood beside her.

"Okfuskee County."

"Woody's stomping grounds."

Jill nodded. "Tiny school. The kids were really into the Eagle play. Pretending to fly, dancing all over the cafeteria, singing." She smiled and then wagged her head. "Throwing the fake fruits and veggies."

"Any casualties?"

"No. But the Head Start teacher intercepted a wicked beet chuck."

"Rackety times," Maytubby said.

"Always." Jill turned to empty a bag of spinach into a strainer. "And to think, I might be crunching epidemiology numbers and sweating tenure."

"In some airless cubby." Maytubby turned on the tap, and she rinsed the spinach. Then she jostled the strainer and set it down.

They lifted their glasses. "To fresh air," she said. They clinked glasses and drank.

Maytubby chopped some pecans. Jill rinsed the whisk and blended raspberry balsamic vinegar and olive oil.

She said, "Dare I ask where you're going in that getup?"

"Out by Ten-Acre Rock."

"East of Mill Creek," Jill said.

"Yes. This afternoon, LeeRoy Sickles led Hannah and me to a charcoal kiln he stumbled on when he was squirrel hunting. Some fifty-gallon drums welded together for burning wood into charcoal. There were charred human remains inside."

"I've never heard of anyone doing that."

"I found one case. In Jamaica." Maytubby set his glass on the table.

"What are you looking for out there?"

"LeeRoy said he thought the kiln, in the woods where he hunted, was on Indian land. I don't know about that yet. He said there was a shack back there occupied by a sketchy couple living off the grid. Also, somebody in a black pickup ran him off the road after he showed Hannah and me the kiln. Hannah got him home."

Jill set salad bowls on the table. "So you're going to climb over that big-ass rock and scamper down to the shack in the dead of night." She glanced down at his trail runners. "Not barefoot this time, like your Tarahumara idols."

"Never say never."

"Sometimes say 'get another shard of glass in your instep and go to the Chickasaw Med Center ER again.'" Jill took a sip of wine. "Wanna get on my computer and search NamUs-dot-gov while the chicken is baking?"

Maytubby blinked, then stared at her. "Oh, man." He hit his forehead with the heel of his hand. "You did that so I couldn't blackmail you with the sorghum."

"Checkmate," she said.

CHAPTER 7

Jill unplugged her laptop while Maytubby freed space on the table. She set it down, opened it, and entered her password. She sat in a chair; Maytubby looked over her shoulder. The NamUs dashboard listed the most recent reports of missing people. She narrowed the search to Oklahoma.

They scanned the case files from the past three days.

Maytubby said, "I think there were melted Converse All Stars in there. So maybe a teenager."

"Plenty of those," Jill said. "Male or female?"

"Won't know until the forensic anthropologist from the state medical examiner's office makes a call. Isn't there a search box for physical characteristics? The jaw had a broken incisor." Maytubby reached over her shoulder and picked up his wineglass.

"Here. Distinctive Physical Features." She typed in "broken incisor." The autofill inserted "or" between the words. She changed it to "and." Only one result appeared. A blurry color photo of a teenage boy with long, straight black hair. To the right of that:

Cyrus "Cy" Mead, Male, Caucasian
Date of Last Contact: three days earlier

Missing From: Cairo, Oklahoma

Missing Age: 16

In unison, Jill and Maytubby said, "That's a Chickasaw name."

Jill said, "I have a vague memory it's anglicized."

"My great-aunt Maytubby lives near Cairo," he said. "Somehow, on a remnant of a Choctaw allotment." Maytubby took out his phone and typed the contact info into his notes.

Jill closed the tabs and shut her laptop. She slumped in her chair. "Poor Cy."

"Dark business," Maytubby said.

Jill carried the laptop away. Then they both stood silent, staring out opposite windows. Satie's single notes rose and fell. The oven whooshed to life.

―――――――――

When they had eaten, Maytubby took their plates and utensils to the sink, filled it with hot water, and added dish soap. Jill lidded the baking dish and put it in the refrigerator. She pulled a dish towel from the fridge handle and moved to the sink. When he handed her the first plate, she rinsed it under the tap and said, "I guess reading club is off the table."

"Yeah. Olive Kitteridge will have to fume alone."

"Squirting her black squid ink." Jill smiled. She dried a plate and set it in the cupboard. "How did you learn to do her Down East voice?"

"Mainer at St. John's." Maytubby swished the cutlery. "Not everybody was from Sheboygan."

Jill dried another plate. "Was the Mainer one of the 'other women' you knew in Santa Fe?"

In a falsetto, Maytubby said, "Ayuh."

Jill laughed and rinsed the silverware, then shook the water on Maytubby.

"Hey!"

"Hey, yourself." She dropped the cutlery in the drainer cup and threaded her towel through a drawer handle.

Maytubby dried his hands on his pants and looked at his watch.

"Zero hour," she said.

"Afraid so."

They moved together and kissed. He snugged his hand over her breast. "Mmmm," she said. They laid their heads on each other's shoulder. The cooling oven popped.

Jill drew back her head. "Text me when you leave the rock."

Maytubby lifted his hat from the chair and donned it. He furtively inserted the goober teeth and smiled at her. "Sure thing."

"Ugh," she said. "Get out of here."

Before he shut the door, she said, "Be safe."

CHAPTER 8

Maytubby switched off the pickup's headlights a quarter mile before he reached Ten-Acre Rock. The moon glinted off the granite chat on the road. The rock materialized from scrub oak forest, blue and lunar. He pulled off the road and killed the engine.

In the faint light, he looked at his field glasses, duty belt, and pistol on the seat, and up at the 20-gauge pump in its ceiling rack. The shotgun would make a good prop—he could pretend to be hunting if he was caught out. But it would slow him down. The pistol was out, too. He was going in without a warrant. He picked up the belt and pistol, leaned forward in the bench seat, pulled the back of the seat against his back, stowed the belt behind the seat, and leaned back slowly. Leave the shotgun? Too alluring. He unracked it and put it behind the seat as well.

He pulled on the cap and seated the Petzl light over its crown. The small field glasses went into his pants pocket. He opened a mapping program on his phone to chart his trip. Years ago, he had removed the cab's overhead lamp. Now he unscrewed the license plate lamp just enough.

Maytubby knew that the approach to the rock was both a country dump and a teenage hangout, strewn with beer cans, campfire rings, rusted bedsprings. He switched on the Petzl and threaded the junk until he hit the base of the rock. Then he switched off the light and climbed by moonlight.

When Maytubby stood at the top, he looked west and saw the streetlamps of Mill Creek. To the north, illuminated quarry conveyor towers and winking strobes atop the wind turbines. South and east, where he was bound, not a single light. Indian Territory outlaws found the rock a useful perch.

He scooted down the other side and walked into the woods. Blackjack oaks shed their leaves late. The canopy was still dense, moonlight venous on the forest floor. He held both hands in front of him as he walked, pushing aside stiff branches. Maytubby remembered that whites scouting this territory for Indian removal had cursed the blackjack Cross Timbers as "forests of cast iron." *Chiskilik.* His grandmother's word for the tree came to him. It was the sound of the branches scraping against his sleeves and snapping back.

He had no idea where the shack was. Every hundred yards or so, he stopped to listen. Distant coyotes and dogs, a quarry train blowing for a crossing, sometimes an owl. While he was on the move, he heard animals scurrying through the fallen leaves—coons, possums, or foxes. He came to stony outcrops, some so steep he had to sit and crab his way down. Prickly pear cactus spines jabbed his heels.

An hour in, stopping to listen, he caught a whiff of charcoal smoke. The breeze was from the southeast. Not likely from the kiln. The swarm of agents would have warned off those folks. Maytubby picked up his pace, the limbs scouring his palms. Soon the charcoal smoke mingled with cooking onions and meat. Still he saw no light.

A few more steps, and Maytubby heard a metallic snap an instant before a jolt of pain hit his forefoot. He pitched forward, breaking the fall with his hands. The coil-spring game trap was chained to a stake. Slowly he turned his head and lowered it into the bed of leaves. Then he lay still, gritted his teeth, and listened. His fall would have carried some hundreds of yards if someone was out and about.

After ten minutes of silence, he felt around for a sturdy fallen oak branch, planted it like a staff, and then climbed it with his hands until he stood. Maytubby had trapped coons and coyotes for their pelts when he was a kid. He worked the drill, set the butt of the stave on one spring lever and his free foot on the other, then heaved down with both until the jaws opened. He freed his trapped foot and let the jaws snap shut.

Cigarette smoke joined the cooking smells. Why couldn't he see a light?

Maytubby leaned on the limb and moved his toes. The trail runner squished with blood, but his bones and tendons held firm. Still, he was loath to abandon the crutch. He hobbled with it for a few hundred yards, backing into the densest thickets when his free hand wasn't enough to protect his face. When the pain grew familiar and tolerable, he laid the branch on the ground and limped toward the smoke.

Soon, a dim light flickered to his right. He tacked and padded softly across the leaves—wincing, taking deep breaths. When the light took the shape of a frame, he pulled the field glasses from his pants pocket and eased down onto an outcrop. The binoculars showed him a lantern burning inside the hut, its mantles waxing and waning. It needed pumping.

What self-respecting crook, even in Bumfuck, Oklahoma, would leave a window unshaded? A *clean* window at that.

He heard at least one hog snorting. Hens would be silent, roosting after dark.

The house was in a very small clearing. Moonlight sharpened its outline and the stovepipe rising from its roof. Blue smoke drifted from the pipe. A crease of light opened, and a figure emerged from the house, faintly backlit. Even in silhouette, the long white hair and full hips clearly belonged to a woman. A match flared, and Maytubby glimpsed a wizened face. She lit a cigarette and shook out the match. The cigarette glowed fat and irregular—a roll-your-own.

In the window, the lantern suddenly brightened. He could see a hand working the plunger. Then the face of a white-bearded man, his eyes narrowed on the task. Soon, the man walked out of the frame. In brighter light, Maytubby saw orderly rows of tools and iron ornaments on the far wall of the room, all hung from forked hooks: sledges, axes, ball-peen hammers, coat hooks. Even at this distance, the irregularity of both the ironwork and the wooden hafts told Maytubby they were homemade. So the hermits ran a cottage industry. That would explain the charcoal kiln and the forge. It would not explain murder.

Artisanal tools might fetch a premium as objets d'art for wealthy young urbanites. If LeeRoy was right about the weird couple riding a motorcycle, those sledges and axes would make for some lumpy saddlebags.

The bearded man joined the smoking woman outside. He carried something in each hand. The woman's cigarette jumped away, making an orange arc. He was bringing food. While they bent their heads over the meal, Maytubby glassed the area behind the house. A small windowless outbuilding near the house he guessed was the jakes. Behind that, forty or so yards away, stood a larger structure, maybe ten by ten. Moonlight glinted off a dark window and showed a stovepipe jutting from a metal roof. There was no smoke.

Maytubby stowed his field glasses and weighed the risks of movement. There was little wind to rustle the leaves and mask his steps. The folks eating their late supper did not speak to each other. So he sat on his rock, running a hand up and down his left thigh to fool the pain in his foot.

He looked up at the moon and thought of his Chickasaw ancestors' god, Aba'Binni'li'. Maytubby had learned the word from his *ippo'si'*, his grandmother. He had read that when a Chickasaw delegation traveled to Savannah in the 1730s to replenish ammo for their war against the French from New Orleans, they had met John Wesley, the founder of Methodism. A translator told him they believed in a superior being who lived with the sun and moon. Maytubby wondered what John Wesley had thought of them. What did they think of him?

The old couple shook their plates and went inside, shutting the front door. He took out his field glasses again, watched them sit at a table. The woman picked up a small object from the table, fiddled with it, and put it back. She extended her hand to the man, who took something from it. She set the object down, and in unison they tilted their heads back and clapped a hand to their mouths. So they were sharing medicine? She lifted a deck of cards from the table, did an overhand shuffle, and set the cards down. Their gestures told him they were talking. The walls and their voices would cover him until the card game began in earnest. If he waited for them to retire for the night, he would lose the moonlight. He pocketed his glasses and rose. The pain freshened, and he winced at the first step toward the far shed.

He trod gently, scouted for a henhouse and coop. Roused hens would undo him. He saw neither and made the back shed, put it between himself and the house before he approached it. He stood still and let his retinas absorb more light.

There was a door on the left, with a serious padlock hanging from a hasp. On the right, a window. He moved close to the glass and cupped his hands around his headlamp before he switched it on. A stained paper roller shade had been pushed tight against the interior frame. He switched off the Petzl and ran his hands over the tar paper nailed to the exterior walls, feeling for a loose patch. He went outward from the door and window frames, first as high as he could reach, on the toes of his good foot, then down on his knees, brailling the paper.

Near the joint of wall and floor, he found a loose flap. He lay on the ground and peeled it back, moved his face close to the wall, and flicked on the lamp. The paper came away easily. Beneath it, the old board-and-batten siding was warped, its nails poking out. Maytubby took hold of one of the narrow vertical battens between the wider boards and gingerly snapped off a foot of it. Lying on his back, he removed the headlamp harness from his hat, pressed the lens against the crack, and switched it on. He moved his eye under the light until he could see inside the shack.

There were several freestanding metal shelves packed with big white stock bottles, all bearing pharmaceutical labels he could not read. He didn't need to. He flicked off the light, snugged its elastic over his cap, tapped the broken batten back into place, and let the tar paper fall over it. That was a lot of medicine for two old people.

He rolled over and moved to get on all fours when he heard a door bang, then loud steps on the leaves. He froze and listened. The steps came toward him, then stopped. He heard a spring creak, then another door slam. One of the old couple was visiting the outhouse. He relaxed and waited. Soon the spring creaked again, the door slammed, and footsteps retreated. When the big house's door shut, he got to his feet and limped slowly away from the buildings, northward. He didn't angle back toward the road for a mile.

By the time Maytubby changed course, waning moonlight darkened the woods. He parried the blackjack limbs blindly with his hands. It was time for the Petzl. Just as he reached for the switch, a bouncing light appeared in the near distance, between him and the road. He pivoted to the right and duckwalked to get under the low branches. His foot throbbed, but crawling would thrash the leaves. Twice he saw the flashlight beam sweep the treetops above him.

When he was farther north, he turned and watched the beam move away from him, toward the house. Then he stood, put out his hands, and limped toward Ten-Acre Rock and his truck.

Even with the low moon, the rock glowed above the forest. Maytubby stopped and listened. Nothing. The person with the flashlight had come from the road. Best not to stand on top of the rock and show himself to anyone who remained at the road. He inserted the goober teeth, pocketed his headlamp, and pulled out the plastic whiskey bottle. Then he bent into the blackjacks around the rock. When he came to the rusted bedsprings, he shook them with his hands, tossed a few beer cans against the granite. Then he sang loudly, slurring his words,

"Cluck old hen was a good old hen; she laid eggs for the railroad men . . ."

Sure enough, there was a pickup in the road—by the looks of it, the very GMC. Maytubby staggered and pretended to swill from the bottle.

Before he made the edge of the road, a man walked around the

GMC and shined a flashlight in his face. Maytubby grimaced to show his fake teeth before he threw his arm over his face and shouted, "Hey!"

"Hey yourself," the man said. He pointed a pistol at Maytubby.

Maytubby threw himself on the gravel, let the bottle fall from his hand. He saw the light sweep over his body.

"What I figgered from lookin' in your truck. Then at your face. Just a drunk Indian."

Milk the slur, Maytubby thought. He tensed his body while the man's feet crunched toward him.

The truck's plate would be missing. Unlikely its registration would be in the glove box. If he fought back, his old Ford would become a mark and he couldn't give chase. He braced for the kick. It came quickly, square in his ribs. He groaned and curled into a fetal position.

"That land is private property. Git back in your truck and never come back here," the man said.

"Yes, sir," Maytubby rasped. He got to his knees and then rose on his good foot. He limped to his pickup. The man chortled. Maytubby unlocked the driver's door and got in. He started the engine, wincing at the pain in his left foot, but let out the clutch too quick so it would die. Keep up the ruse. He restarted the pickup and turned on its headlights. When he backed into the road, he was rewarded with a limelight mugshot of the joker who had kicked him. Five six or seven, medium build, red goatee, blue eyes, snaggletooth, black ball cap, sweatshirt with Confederate Stars and Bars. The GMC's right front fender bore the damage from LeeRoy's truck, and the plate was still missing. A silver dealer decal, on the tailgate. Maytubby squinted. "PLAINSMAN" was all he could catch.

Renaldo had lost the GMC at the Samson quarry siding. Maytubby, working the clutch with his right foot when he could, drove the six miles there. The conveyor towers were brightly lit, so he backed his truck into a stand of red cedars. If Redhead had phoned his pal and called him off, they would appear soon. If not, Maytubby would have a long wait. He drank water from his bottle, polished off the Bosc pear and pecans. He leaned against the driver's side door and raised his game foot onto the bench seat. Then he bent his torso to relieve the pain in his ribs.

The grade crossing lights came to life. An engine lugged a short string of sand-laden hopper cars toward the trunk line. After the cars had passed, he looked at the sinking moon and gave himself a half hour before he could no longer tail the GMC without his headlights.

The half hour passed, then more hours. Orion wheeled up the southern sky. Maytubby shifted his body every few minutes to cut the throbbing. Where had the bastards gone?

The GMC roared over the crossing, briefly leaving the ground, and sped west. Maytubby pivoted on the seat and started the engine. Forgetting about his left foot, he drove it into the clutch pedal. The pain shot all the way into his nostrils.

There was no moonlight. Maytubby pushed the Ford's big V-8 and gained on the GMC, following its left and right turns as it skirted the quarry. He had to stay closer than he should so the GMC's taillights kept him on the road. Soon, he and the Jimmy were on Chadwick Road, south of Sulphur. When the GMC's brake lights flashed, he braked as well and watched the truck turn off the road. He crept past the dirt driveway and watched the GMC stop in front of the darkened house. Its headlights lit a decrepit upright farmhouse with no wing, and a seventies-vintage red Chevy pickup parked in the drive. Maytubby did a double take when he saw, an instant before the headlights went off, a constellation of nicks in the GMC's windshield. He gritted his teeth and shifted into second, letting his pickup slide forward almost at an idle until a light came on in the house. Then he turned on his headlights, shifted into third, and drove north one mile to State 7.

He stopped and idled on a treeless knob on the Rock Prairie. Strobes on cell towers and wind turbines blinked in the distance. There was no cover for him anywhere, and he was in no shape to run across a mile of cactus and cobbles to spy on the house.

———————————

Just before dawn, Maytubby limped into the ER at Chickasaw Nation Medical Center on Stonecipher Boulevard in Ada. He produced his driver's license and Chickasaw citizenship card and was shown to an exam room. He removed his bloody left trail runner and sock and mounted the exam table. The wound, above his big toe, still bled. He limped to the paper towel dispenser, pulled out a handful, and wrapped it ugly around his foot. Back on the exam table, he took off his jacket and shirt and tossed them over a chair. The left side of his chest was swollen and starting to bruise.

There was a timid knock on the door, and a sleepy young woman entered carrying an open laptop. She had long black hair and wore a white medical coat. Her name tag said REBECCA HARJO, PA. A Creek name. "Hi," she said, setting the laptop on a desk. She frowned at his foot. Then at his chest. "Mr. Maytubby."

He nodded. "Bill."

"Bill." She snapped two nitrile gloves from a dispenser and pulled them on. Then she quickly took his temperature and blood pressure and pulse, listened to his heart. She glanced at the laptop screen. "Still no meds?" she asked.

"No," he said.

"Fifty-four—you have an athlete's pulse," she said. She spread her hand to indicate his whole body. "This all police work?"

"Just a midnight stroll in the woods. Stepped in a game trap and fell on a rock."

She nodded but shot him a skeptical glance. "Okay. Let's get to work."

––––––––––

Two hours later, Maytubby blinked into the morning sun. The crutches he was forced to take, he dropped into his truck bed. They clinked on the hooch bottles. X-rays had shown no broken bones. PA Harjo had stitched up his foot. He declined narcotics but accepted her offer of ibuprofen tablets. He would need them for his clutch foot until he traded the pickup for the Lighthorse cruiser.

In the cab, he called Jill.

"Home is the hunter," she said. "Any the worse for the wear?"

"A little. Got some stitches in my great toe."

"Your great toe. Nobody says that."

He looked at his stained trail runner. "It sounds more important than 'big toe.'"

"Going Tarahumara commando I guess," she said. He heard coffee percolating.

"No," he said. "I took your advice and wore trail runners. Stepped in a game trap. You spared me a broken phalanx."

"Oh, God."

Maytubby laughed.

"You're in the ER at the med center, then," Jill said.

"Was. On my way to pick up a prisoner in Sulphur." Maytubby gritted his teeth, depressed the clutch, and started the truck.

"In those cretinous teeth and duds?"

"The folksy touch. People like it."

"In a pig's eye," Jill said.

"Hey, I can use that today!"

"You do that."

"Where does the anti-sugar legion march today?" Maytubby said.

"Stringtown." She paused a second. "And no rampart jokes."

"Damn. Now I'm just an old shoe."

Jill laughed. "Off we go."

"Off we go."

Maytubby drove to his house, changed into his uniform, retrieved the duty belt and pistol from behind the pickup seat, and lifted the shotgun into its overhead rack. He threw all the whiskey bottles back into the well and leaned his crutches on the porch railing.

On the way to Lighthorse headquarters, he bought a large coffee and a pumpkin muffin at Hot Shots. In the police lot, he parked near his cruiser so he could hobble to it unseen by Sheila and Chief Fox. He nestled the coffee cup into place and set the muffin sack on the passenger seat.

Fifteen miles down the road, the coffee failed. He pulled into a shallow turnout, flicked on his strobes, set the timer on his phone to twenty minutes, and turned on his mobile data terminal. Its screen blazed to life an instant before he fell dead asleep.

He was startled awake by loud raps on his window. His cell promptly chimed in.

CHAPTER 9

Hannah Bond had slept three hours before she awoke in her bed without an alarm. She put on her uniform over the boxers and T-shirt she slept in, buckled on her duty belt, walked to her kitchen, and fried three eggs and three slices of bacon as she watched traffic on US 377 out her window.

She walked two blocks to the Johnston County Courthouse and filled a Styrofoam cup with burnt coffee from the Sheriff's Department urn. The sheriff waved at her as she collected two summonses for addresses north of Tishomingo. She liked to serve them early in the morning, before people had time to make a plan.

After she had served the summonses, she recognized Maytubby's Lighthorse cruiser by its number. It was parked off the road, its overheads flashing. She parked behind it and hit her strobes as well. Maytubby's black hair was mashed against the driver's window. She knocked hard on the glass.

Maytubby bolted up and stared at her. Then he frowned and reached for his cell on the passenger seat. He fiddled with it and stuck it in his pocket. Bond stepped back as he opened the cruiser's door. Maytubby's eyes were swollen.

"Hannah," he said. They walked together away from the traffic. Maytubby's game foot was stiff.

"I never known you to sleep on the job, Bill." She paused. "Fact is, I never seen you limp except when you stepped on that Choc bottle after I shot Hillers at Nail's Crossing."

Maytubby smiled weakly. "I was wearing shoes, stepped in a spring trap when I was scouting that shack LeeRoy mentioned. Got stitched up at CNMC."

"You see anything out there?" Hannah stuck her thumbs in her duty belt and watched the highway over Maytubby's shoulder.

"Like LeeRoy said, an old hippie couple roughing it. Looked like they make tools by hand. Axes and froes and such. Maybe to sell to folk-art collectors."

Bond snorted. "Well, you moved among rich folks in college. You would know about nimrods who waste their money on somethin' they could buy cheap at the lumberyard."

Maytubby stifled the urge to scuff his left foot on the gravel.

"How'd you see in that shack?" Hannah said.

"No shades on the windows. Nighttime."

"Huh." Bond turned her head to watch northbound traffic. "Not like crooks."

"No."

"The tools would explain the kiln and the forge, but not the dead body."

Maytubby rolled his head around and hunched his shoulders. "I found a shed back of the house. Stocked with big white pill bottles."

"Ah," Bond said.

"When I got back to the pickup, that Jimmy was waiting for me. And so was . . ." Maytubby paused and looked at Hannah. "Wait."

Bond nodded and half-smiled. "You saw the windshield."

"LeeRoy," Maytubby said. "His ten gauge."

"Ho-ho. Yeah."

"You were at his place last night."

"But *I* got home in time to sleep," Hannah said.

"Two guys."

"Yup. The bigger one came at the house with a long gun and a entry ram. He was wearin' a princess mask. A scritch owl spooked him right before I did. He dropped the ram and took off. That's when LeeRoy let fly."

"The smaller guy's a redhead," Maytubby said. "He was standing by the GMC, armed, when I came out of the woods. I had bought a half-pint of whiskey in Ada and made like I had got drunk on the Rock. Pitched myself down on the road."

"Don't tell me," Hannah said.

"I didn't think of that until just before he said it. He kicked me in the ribs but let me drive away."

"Maggot." Hannah lowered her face a little. "You catch the dealer sticker name?"

"All I could read was 'Plainsman.'"

"Good," Hannah nodded.

"I drove to the railroad crossing where Renaldo lost the GMC. It showed up, and I followed it to an old farmhouse on Chadwick Road. Seventies red Chevy pickup parked there. I'll text you the satellite map."

"They'll either fix the windshield in Sulphur today or start drivin' the Chevy."

"One more thing, Hannah. Jill searched NamUs and found a missing sixteen-year-old boy with a chipped front tooth. Chickasaw name—Mead. Missing three days ago from Cairo, just outside Coalgate."

"You're cross-deputized in the Choctaw Nation." Hannah resumed watching southbound traffic.

"I am," Maytubby said. "But right now I have to pick up one of my own citizens from the Murray County lockup and take him to Pontotoc."

Hannah turned her face to Maytubby and then looked away from the road. "Pay no attention to the road."

Maytubby turned his back on it. A car slowed and then accelerated, headed south.

"I saw a fat head in a white Charger," she said.

"Scrooby."

"Nobody but. On his way back to the crime scene."

They stared at a roadside stand of hackberry trees. Maytubby said, "You know an oil patch field landman in Tish?"

"Goin' around your boss, huh?"

Maytubby smiled at her.

"I know a female field landman in Tish. You want her to find out if LeeRoy's right about that being Indian land."

"Yes," Maytubby said. "She could go to the Johnston County Courthouse and look at the old Dawes book. Find the name on the original allotment and then see if someone else owns the land now."

"You payin'?"

"Yeah. For an hour's work." He took out his wallet and handed her three twenties—all the cash he had. "I'm acting as a curious civilian."

Hannah took the bills and said, "She'll have to do what you're doin': hide it from her boss. A broker, I think he's called. *That's* the feller makes the foldin' money."

"You got time today?"

"I'll hide it from *my* boss." Hannah turned toward her cruiser, and Maytubby limped behind her. "We're a reg'lar crime ring, Bill."

"We should arrest us."

Maytubby drove toward Sulphur. Bond slid into her cruiser and glanced at the summonses. The work she'd done would buy her an hour. She skirted Tishomingo on county roads and drove down Pecan Bottom Road. The nut harvest was afoot, tractor-mounted tree shakers thrumming in the groves. She pulled into a short driveway leading to a small, neat frame house with a yaupon hedge. A mud-spattered elderly Ford pickup was parked in the yard.

She knocked on the door. It was opened by a short woman with graying blond hair cropped close. "Hannah! Come in." Bond stepped inside and heard the door shut quickly behind her. The woman stepped in front of her and motioned her to a chair at a small kitchen table. There was a small laptop and a stack of papers on one edge. Hannah could see columns of typewritten text and numbers on the top paper. It was headed "Tract Index."

"Patty," Bond said as she sat.

Patty scurried to the kitchen counter and poured two cups of coffee from a drip decanter. She set them on the table and sat across from Bond. "I haven't seen you since our food pantry days." Her face drooped. "Poor Alice." She fidgeted. "I heard you caught her killer down on the Washita."

Bond sipped her coffee. "I had some help."

"That tribal cop."

"Bill Maytubby," Bond said.

Patty nodded slowly and drank some coffee. Her eyes swiveled. She set her hands on the table, jumped up, opened a drawer under the countertop, and rattled some silverware. Then she returned to the table and sat, fidgeting.

"I remember you were livin' with a girlfriend," Hannah said.

Patty frowned and looked down, then up at Hannah. "Oh, she took off six months ago. Gone with the wind." She waved her hand.

"I'm sorry, Patty."

"Me, too, Hannah." Patty's eyes reddened. She said in a thick voice, "It's the way of the world. Good woman, too." She cleared her throat. "Anyway, what can I do you for?"

Bond said, "Patty, Bill and me are looking into another killing. Up by Ten-Acre Rock."

"I know where that is," Patty said. She ran a hand through her hair and pulled at an earlobe.

"We think it may be Indian land. We need to know the name of the original allottee and who owns the land now. Can you do it with GPS coordinates?"

Patty frowned and seemed to write on the table with her index finger. Then she tapped the tabletop, looked up at Bond, and smiled. She put her hands in her lap. "So. The Lighthorse Police could get this from the Chickasaw Nation. You want to get ahead of 'em."

"Yeah," Bond said. "I'm on my lunch hour. Not official Sheriff's Department business."

"Nothing illegal I can think of. I may have to wear a wig and sunglasses so my boss doesn't see me going to the courthouse."

Bond smiled. "We can pay you."

"Bullshit." Patty waved her hand. "You took down Alice's killer. This's on the house."

"Thanks," Bond said. She pulled her cell out of her pocket and showed Patty the photo and the pin with the GPS coordinates for the property. Patty leaned into the phone. She gave Bond her cell number. "Send it to me."

Bond did.

Patty checked her phone. She laid it next to her laptop and began tapping. "I'm entering the coordinates into Google Maps—degrees, minutes, and seconds." She hit a key and watched the screen. "Here we go," she said, and swiveled the screen toward Bond. "Does this look right?"

Hannah leaned over the table and peered at the screen. "That's the spot," she said.

Patty returned the computer to its place and nodded to Hannah. "I can find this in the county clerk's index. Take it from there. Should be quick." Patty rose and strode to the front door. Bond stood up and followed her.

At the front door, Hannah said, "I'm sorry about your friend."

Patty nodded. Before she shut the door, she shrugged on a jacket and said, "I'll call you in an hour, Hannah."

Bond drove to a promising speeder patch near the crime scene—State 1 south of Mill Creek. She parked her cruiser in a turnout. She radioed the dispatcher, told her the summonses had been served, and relayed her position.

Two OSBI cars passed her going toward the crime scene before her radar marked a silver sedan doing ninety. After the driver signed her citation, Bond saw an Oklahoma Highway Patrol cruiser going the same direction. She and Renaldo caught each other's eye at the last second and waved.

She cited two more speeders before her cell phone hummed with Patty's call.

"Hey," Bond said. "Can I record this?"

"Sure," Patty said. She waited.

"Okay, shoot," Bond said.

"At the courthouse, I looked at the county clerk tract index, then at the patent book. The land was a forty-acre allotment granted by the Chickasaw Nation after the feds had abolished communal land in the late 1800s. The grantee was Augustus Mead. The type of grant was a homestead patent. Signed by the Chickasaw governor."

Bond clicked her radar off and turned her eyes away from the highway.

"The patent is a type called 'restricted interest,' which means it can't be changed without a court order. Then I visited the Dawes Commission book, which has the nitty-gritty in handwriting. Augustus was forty-three years old, a full-blood Chickasaw. Last thing. I looked at the assessor's map, and the land remains tax exempt. That land still belongs to the descendants of the allottee, Augustus Mead. In all my days as a landman, I've never seen anything like it."

"That patch must've never caught an oil outfit's interest," Bond said.

"Maybe, Hannah, but not much oil patch action around there." Patty was silent a moment. "What does this mean?"

"I don't know, yet, Patty. There are people living on that land, and I don't think they're Indians."

"Squatters, you think?"

"I don't know," Hannah said.

"White people have done that. The fancy term is adverse possession. They have to live on the land fifteen years running. It's the owner's responsibility to kick 'em off."

"Is that so," Hannah said. A truck roared past, and when she saw it was not the GMC, she listened again.

"You think the squatters had something to do with the murder?" Patty said.

"We're gonna find out, Patty. Thank you for doin' this so quick."

"Easy as fallin' off a log. One more thing. I noticed that many acres of land adjoining the Mead property on three sides is owned by someone named Mitchell Searcy. Ring a bell?"

"No," Hannah said. "But it sounds dodgy. You'd make a fine detective, Patty."

"Not on your life."

CHAPTER 10

Maytubby pulled his cruiser off Oklahoma Avenue in Sulphur, across the street from the Oklahoma School for the Deaf. On his phone he searched for auto glass shops in town. There were five. The Murray County Sheriff's Department expected him to pick up his prisoner in a half hour. He mapped his route in his head, the most distant auto glass shop from the courthouse first, the nearest last.

The cruiser would spook his crooks, so he parked a half block from each store and scanned it with his field glasses. No sign of the GMC at the first four. He checked his watch. Eight minutes. The last store was only two blocks from the courthouse.

It was a turquoise cinder-block building surrounded by junk cars and piles of shattered windshields, their severed black molding twisting up like snakes. The GMC was parked out front. As he had hoped, Red and Princess had reattached the license plate to keep off the Sulphur cops. Maytubby typed the number into his phone notes. A young man wearing a dirty Texas Rangers cap stood on a wooden stool and worked a gasket locking tool. The job was almost complete. Maytubby saw no sign of the crooks, backed away from the shop, and drove to the Murray County jail. Deputies would see the cruiser and know he had arrived on schedule.

He got on his cruiser's computer and ran the tag. It was reported stolen from a vehicle in Ravia, Johnston County. If he informed the deputies and had the driver—by Bond's account, Princess—arrested, he could be identified and locked up. Bond's testimony would get him charged in the assault on Sickles's house. Princess's sidekick would find his way back to the house on Chadwick Road and get behind the wheel of the red Chevy pickup.

Maytubby found it useful to let crooks run until they flushed bigger game. Should he let them both run, or was Red good enough? *Was* there bigger game? He checked his rearview mirror and saw the GMC flash by on Broadway, headed east. It would be out of the county before he made it through the courthouse door.

His prisoner sat listless in the back seat, shackled and reeking of sweat and tobacco. Maytubby radioed Lighthorse headquarters in Ada.

"Hey, Bill."

"Hey, Sheila. Got the prisoner in Sulphur. En route to Pontotoc lockup."

"'On root'? You pullin' my leg?"

The prisoner chortled.

Maytubby had forgotten to code-switch. He started the cruiser and eased onto Wyandotte Avenue. "Just trying to class things up."

"That's jackass," Sheila said.

The prisoner laughed out loud.

"Have him up there right quick," Maytubby said.

"That's better," she said.

The prisoner lost interest. His head lolled on his shoulder, and he started to snore. Maytubby drove east on State 7, tracing the GMC's likely route. As he neared Chadwick Road, he checked his mirror to make sure the prisoner was asleep. He braked gently and turned onto the dirt road. Nearing the old farmhouse, he slowed just a little. The GMC was parked in the yard, its stolen plate still attached. The red Chevy pickup was gone. Maytubby rejoined State 1 north of Mill Creek. He spotted Hannah's cruiser, switched on his strobes, and parked behind her. His prisoner slumbered on.

Hannah unfolded herself from her cruiser as Maytubby opened his door quietly and left his engine running. They walked into the bar ditch together. "Hey, Rip," she said.

Maytubby smiled. He jerked a thumb toward his cruiser and spoke softly. "Prisoner's asleep."

Hannah looked over his shoulder. She nodded.

"I checked the auto glass places in Sulphur," Maytubby said. "Found the GMC, with a plate stolen from Ravia. It got around me when I was at Murray lockup, just saw it back home on my way here. Plate still on it." He looked back at his cruiser.

Hannah tucked her thumbs into her duty belt. "I got some news for us. My friend the woman landman went to the Johnston courthouse. LeeRoy was right. It's Indian land. She found the original whatchacallit, grant or—"

"Patent?" Maytubby said.

"Yeah, that. Full-blood Chickasaw named Augustus Mead. Same last name as the missing kid. Still in his name. Still tax exempt, too."

"Rare," Maytubby said.

"Exactly what Patty—the landman—said." Hannah pointed at his cruiser. "Your prisoner woke up."

Maytubby turned, waved his hand at the car, and turned back to Hannah. "You told her about the squatters?"

"Yeah. She said they had to stay on the land fifteen years to claim it."

"LeeRoy said they'd been there a coon's age," Maytubby said.

"She also said a guy named Searcy owns a lot of land on three sides of the Indian land."

"So maybe the Chickasaw land is a keystone," Maytubby said.

"A what?" Hannah said.

"The top stone that finishes an arch or bridge."

"Hey!" the prisoner shouted from the cruiser.

"Hold on!" Maytubby said. To Hannah he said, "I'm off tomorrow. But I have to sleep after my shift."

"I'm off, too. By the way . . ." She reached into her shirt pocket and pulled out his twenties. "Patty wouldn't take your money. Because we got Alice's killer."

Maytubby slid the bills into his wallet.

Hannah pointed vaguely in the direction of Ten-Acre Rock. "I bet Scrooby and Magaw arrested the people in that shack. The axe-makers."

"The squatters."

Maytubby and Bond walked away from each other.

When Maytubby slid into his cruiser, his prisoner said, "I gotta piss."

Maytubby got back out, opened the rear door, led the prisoner into the bar ditch, and unlocked his handcuffs.

While the prisoner fumbled at his fly, he said, "Where the hell you takin' me?" He breathed loudly as he peed. "And while we're at it, who is Miz Godzilla?"

Maytubby waited for him to zip up and place his hands behind his back. When the cuffs were on and they were walking back to the cruiser, Maytubby said, "Mr. Cross, I'm taking you to Pontotoc. That was police business. And the officer was Hannah Bond, the best marksman in the state. I saw her knock a fleeing killer off his motorcycle with an antique revolver." He put his hand on the prisoner's head and eased him into the cruiser's back seat.

Maytubby drove north under the flickering shadows of wind turbine blades.

After he had dropped off his prisoner at the Pontotoc County jail, Maytubby drove to Lighthorse Police headquarters.

Sheila said, "Well, if it ain't Mr. On Root."

"Big as life and twice as ugly," Maytubby said. He handed her the transfer paperwork.

She grinned and took the papers, glanced down at his leg. "Why're you gimp?"

"Ingrown toenail," Maytubby said.

"Right." Sheila rolled her eyes. "Chief Fox—"

He nodded.

Fox motioned Maytubby into his office and handed him a summons.

"Why are you favoring that leg?" Fox said.

"Ingrown toenail."

Fox nodded and said, "Bill, I haven't heard back from the nation about who owns the kiln-corpse land. Scrooby got a search warrant. His forensic anthropologist has taken the skeleton to the state medical examiner's office. There was an old hippie couple living in a shack near the kiln. Apparently, they used the kiln to make charcoal to forge homemade axes and such. Also, Scrooby's agents found an outbuilding behind the house packed with OxyContin. OSBI confiscated the drugs and took them to the City. Scrooby obtained an arrest warrant and told Sheriff Magaw to grab the old hippies for possession of Schedule II with intent to distribute."

Maytubby looked at the summons and said nothing. He didn't want Fox to see his eyes.

Fox was silent for a beat. Then he said, "Scrooby told Magaw this morning that Trooper Renaldo had reported a GMC pickup running LeeRoy Sickles off the road. Scrooby's investigator talked with Sickles because he found the corpse. Sickles told him the GMC came to his house late last night and Sickles shot at the pickup with his elephant gun." Maytubby glanced up for an instant and saw Fox smile and shake his head. "The pickup drove away. Sickles showed the investigator an entry ram the GMC driver dropped in his yard. I don't know what to make of that."

Maytubby turned the summons over in his hands. So LeeRoy had not told the OSBI agent that Hannah was there. Maytubby waited for Fox to ask him what he knew. A wall clock next to the governor's picture ticked off the seconds.

Fox walked back to his desk and sat down. Maytubby looked up and saw that he was eyeing his computer screen. Fox did not look at Maytubby's face but waved a hand toward the summons. "That's on

Bullet Prairie Road. Pontotoc told Sheila they had Cross in custody. Enjoy your days off."

Maytubby left the chief's office and walked to the dispatcher's desk. Sheila hung up her desk phone and said, "You must be *on root* to Bullet Prairie."

"I'm headed there, yeah." He smiled and gave her a little salute.

"Enjoy your days off. Love to Jill." She gave him a 1940s movie wink.

Maytubby called Hannah on his cell before he started his cruiser.

"Hey, Bill. Call you in five. Writing up a speeder."

"Okay."

Maytubby drove back down State 1. Fox had given him a second assignment near the crime scene. Was he paying out leash?

When Maytubby's phone buzzed, he pulled to the shoulder and switched on his overheads. "Yeah, Hannah."

"The GMC passed me going south a half hour ago. Mindin' the limit. Not headed toward LeeRoy's place."

"Speaking of," Maytubby said, "I just talked to Fox. From what he told me, LeeRoy didn't tell Scrooby's investigator you were at his house last night."

"Well, I'll be switched. Good for him. I told him I'd tell Magaw and Scrooby what happened. Then I figured Scrooby and his folks would find him with computers on their own. So I kept quiet."

"LeeRoy packs some cunning," Maytubby said.

"Along with that ten gauge."

"And you were right, Hannah. Scrooby had Magaw arrest the squatters. For the Oxy. They're in Johnston County lockup. OSBI confiscated the drugs."

"You think Princess and Red know about either one?"

"Good question," Maytubby said. "Maybe they were too busy fixing LeeRoy's mischief."

"They should of split up so one could take the red truck and keep watch. Stupid is as stupid does."

"I have a summons to deliver on Bullet Prairie Road," Maytubby said. "Then I have to sleep. You want to go to Cairo with me in the morning so we can talk to my great-aunt Maytubby, who lives close to Cy Mead's folks? Maybe visit some burgled pharmacies?"

"My house is closer. We'll take the Skylark. We might get lucky, run into the maggots along the way. And Red knows your truck."

"Seven okay?" Maytubby said.

"You'll have to tote your own rabbit food."

"Nuts and berries, you mean."

Hannah moved toward her cruiser and half-turned toward him. "I'll bring some Slim Jims, case we get into another firefight."

———————————

Maytubby delivered his summons to a frightened man in striped boxers who signed with an *X* and slammed the door of his wheelless travel trailer.

Bullet Prairie Road ended a few miles short of Ten-Acre Rock. Maytubby parked and turned off his cruiser. The barbed wire fence in front of him, strung loosely on makeshift blackjack posts, had a slug-riddled sign that said, "KEEP OUT THIS MEANS YOU."

He couldn't display the cruiser at the crime scene access or at the partiers' turnout at the Rock. Princess and Red might be parked at either place. And he didn't know if Scrooby's team would still be working the site. His ribs and foot ached.

Chief Fox had turned a blind eye to this chance. It would be a shame to waste it.

Maytubby pocketed his field glasses, removed his Smokey hat, and threw it on the passenger seat. He scanned the road. Then he limped to the fence, lay on the ground, held up the bottom strand of wire, and rolled under it. His ribs hit stones. He stood and walked. The first few dozen steps caught his breath up short. Across a clearing, he quickened his gait. By the time he reached blackjack timber and set his hands against its iron lattice, he could ignore the pain.

An hour later, he spotted the outbuilding a hundred yards off. He

TEN-ACRE ROCK · 63

lay prone behind a stump and glassed the shed. Segments of yellow crime scene tape littered the ground. It should be strung between trees. If Scrooby had closed the crime scene, his troops would have taken it down and removed it.

The rear door was open a crack, its padlock missing. Scrooby would have broken it off. Maytubby watched the shed and listened. A few crows squawked as they juked overhead. In the distance, a quarry train blew, likely for the Samson Road crossing.

Something moved, down the hill on his right. He slowly moved his binoculars. A lone whitetail buck cantered away from him. Rut was almost over, and the fellow was gaunt from chasing and mounting does.

Loud voices erupted from the shed. The buck's ears flicked up and he bounded away. Maytubby turned his glasses to the shed. He heard some crashing and violent oaths.

The shed door opened slowly, and a man's face appeared from the dark interior. Not Red's; someone taller than Red. The man stepped from the shed and surveyed the woods. He motioned with his arm, and Red stepped out. They stood still for a few seconds. Both wore sidearms. Then they bent at their waists and walked slowly northeast, toward Ten-Acre Rock. Their heads swiveled, and they kept their palms on their pistols. Soon they were jogging away.

Maytubby stowed his field glasses. He grimaced as he got to his knees and then stood. Princess and Red owed pills to their desperate clients. They needed fresh inventory.

An hour later, Maytubby rolled back under the barbed wire and got in his cruiser. He drained the last of his coffee, logged on to his computer, and scanned OSBI's database of recent Part 1 crimes—the bad ones. He checked for pharmacy robberies and burglaries within fifty miles. He found one in Coalgate, one in Allen, and one in Stratford. All were late-night break-ins. Damage indicated an entry ram. Princess and Red now might have to make shift with a different tool.

Maytubby turned off his computer and drove toward headquarters. Turbines in the new wind field glowed pink in the late sun. Hundreds of rescue horses grazed beneath them. He phoned Trooper Renaldo.

"Hey, Bill."

"Hey, Jake. Where are you?"

"Down on the Red. Love County. I heard about Magaw arresting the old hippies by Ten-Acre Rock."

"Yeah," Maytubby said. "Listen, OSBI confiscated a bunch of opioids in a shed there. Long story, but I think the stash belonged to the black GMC pickup folks. I found a few recent pharmacy break-ins in your troop area."

"You're telling me there may be more real soon," Renaldo said.

"Yes. And that the GMC guys—a tall fellow and a short red-head—also have a seventies-model red pickup. The Jimmy has a stolen plate now, but you saw the silver dealer decal on the tailgate. It says 'Plainsman.' Probably—"

"Ardmore dealership," Renaldo said.

"Yeah. Hannah and I are off tomorrow."

Renaldo laughed. "Moonlighting again. Where?"

"Your miner ancestor Giacomo's neck of the woods," Maytubby said.

"Ah. Coalgate. Still some beautiful Italian women walking over those dead shafts."

Maytubby felt a pang of conscience. One of those women was Lorenza Mercante. She owned a liquor store in Coalgate, on a busy state highway. He had dropped in five years ago to ask about a suspect living across the street from her store. She had been a keen observer and helped him solve the case. She had also pulled up her long black hair in her hands and let it fall on her shoulders. Twice more, in the years since, he had returned, with divided motives. Her business and location made Lorenza Mercante a valuable scout. Her frank but sub-dued overtures threw him off kilter. He'd made his engagement clear.

"Lorenza Mercante, for one," Maytubby said, to make a semi-clean breast of it.

"Oh God, yes," Jake said. "She's my second cousin, you know."

"I didn't. She helped me solve a case." Maytubby slowed for a pickup towing a cattle trailer.

"I'll rib her about it at the next family reunion. Dispatch coming in. Talk to you mañana, Bill."

Maytubby parked his cruiser at headquarters and did not go inside. He climbed into his pickup, winced as he clutched it into gear.

Maytubby limped across his plank porch, yanked a few bills out of his mailbox, and let himself inside. He tossed the bills on his kitchen table. Then he set his hands on the table to take some weight off his feet. The house was dark. The thought of his bed, just twenty paces away, made him dizzy.

His phone buzzed. He kept one arm braced on the table. "Hey, Jill Milton."

The line was silent for a few seconds. "You're slurring, Bill. Are you all right?"

"Yeah. Just need to sleep."

"Want me to run over there and keep you warm in that saggy old bed?" Jill said.

"Won't be any fun."

"Don't kid yourself."

"I flunked self-deception," Maytubby said. "Porch light's on."

He limped to his bathroom, pulled off his left shoe and sock, and fumbled fresh dressing onto his foot. After swallowing two aspirin, he got to his bedroom, draped his duty belt on a chairback. He switched on the bedside lamp, plugged his phone into its charger, and laid it on top of Emily Dickinson. "Sleep is the station grand," he quoted her to himself. As he fell back on the bed, in full uniform save for one shoe, he imagined the vaulted ceiling of a Victorian railway station thronged with passengers. Then he was out.

CHAPTER 11

Bond turned in her cruiser at the Johnston County Courthouse and walked the few blocks home in fading sunlight. She changed into jeans and a flannel shirt. In her refrigerator she found a leftover pork chop and a boiled red potato. While she brewed coffee, she stood at her kitchen sink and salted the potato, watching traffic on US 377 through her window. She ate the potato in three bites, salted the chop, and ate that in four. She dropped the bone in the trash, on top of yesterday's squirrel bones. Princess and Red would leave LeeRoy alone now. His house would have drawn the law, and they had bigger fish to fry.

Bond filled a thermos with coffee. She checked the satellite photo of Princess's house Maytubby had sent to her phone. Then she donned an old Oklahoma City 89ers baseball cap and a cotton hoodie, picked up her Steiner binoculars and duty belt, and walked to her rust-stitched Buick Skylark. She stowed her duty belt under the passenger side of the bench seat.

A half hour later, as she neared the house, she slowed and switched off her headlights. Moonlight silvered the road. As she drove past the house, she saw that the porch light was on. The windows were dark. Both trucks were parked in the yard. She drove a quarter mile, made a U-turn, then backed into a ranch driveway that gave her a good view of the house.

She cracked her window and drank coffee from the thermos mouth. A south wind kicked up, rustling the prairie grass. Bond closed her window. She thought of the dead Mead boy, if that was him in the kiln. Not much older than her little sister when she was raped and stabbed to death by one of their foster fathers in a shack in the Ouachitas.

An hour passed. Bond scanned the house with her Steiners. Nothing. She laid them on her seat and drank more coffee. The wind picked up. No vehicles passed.

Just past midnight, the porch light shuddered. Bond raised her binoculars and saw two forms running off the porch and making for the bigger truck, the GMC. She couldn't hear it start, but its reverse lights blazed and moved toward the road. She waited for the driver to shift into a forward gear before she started the Skylark. But the reverse lights stayed lit. They sped toward her, the pickup weaving. Now she heard the keening of a strained reverse gear.

"Well, shit," she said. She started her engine and shifted into first. Before she could pop the clutch, the pickup's rear steel bumper rammed her grille. In the red reflection of the truck's taillights, she saw two men jump from the cab. One disappeared behind the passenger fender. The other, carrying a flashlight, bent to the ground outside her window. The flashlight lit her face an instant before something smashed her window and struck her jaw. She felt the object graze her thigh and heard it thump on the floorboard.

The flashlight beam danced around the cabin and returned to her face. She smelled chaw on his breath. "Hey, Timbo!" he shouted in her face. "Ain't no kids fuckin' in this car. Just a old sow." He spat on her cheek. The face withdrew. "No kicks to be had here. We got work to do."

The man under her fender rose and jogged to the passenger door of the pickup. The flashlight went out, and the man at her window stepped to the driver's side of the pickup. When the truck lurched away, its trailer hitch pulled the Skylark's bumper molding away. The truck's brake lights flashed, and the driver jumped out of the cab, ran behind the tailgate, and yanked the bumper molding loose. It clattered into the bar ditch. He returned to the truck and revved its engine. Gravel rained on the Skylark as the GMC hurtled into the dark.

Bond wiped the stinking spittle off her cheek with her left hand. Another flashback to her foster father's lips, glistening with tobacco juice. His leering smile just before he spat on her sister's limp body.

With her right hand, Bond turned the ignition key. When she released the clutch, the old Buick lunged. Then it bumped and stalled. She growled and brushed broken glass off her jeans. Moonlight glinted off shards that had stuck to her hands. She opened her thermos and rinsed off the glass with warm coffee.

She reached under the passenger seat, pulled her duty belt into her lap, slid out the Maglite, and set the belt atop her Steiners. She flicked on the light. Blood from her cheek dripped slowly onto her jeans. She found the stone and threw it out the broken window, opened the door and jacked the window crank clockwise to lower the intact glass and knock the shards onto the ground.

She shut the door, walked to the front of the car and inspected the grille. The GMC had not punctured the radiator. Under the passenger side fender, she saw that her tire had been slashed.

She hefted out the spare from the trunk, rolled it around the car, returned to the trunk, and collected a rusted bumper jack and an L-shaped lug wrench. The bumper molding was gone. She knelt on the ground, located a place on the bottom of the solid bumper for the jack's cradle. Then she set up the jack standard bar and went to work.

Before the tire cleared the ground, she heard a moaning sound behind the car. She scrambled up and pointed the Maglite. The pipe gate to the ranch was slowly opening. She had heard its hinges. Now she heard the electric swing-gate motor. She raised the light and saw a man with a shotgun in the crook of his left arm walking toward the open gate. Then she was blinded by his flashlight.

Bond shielded her eyes with her free hand but kept the Maglite aimed at the man. His Western boots crunched on the graveled driveway. He walked through the gate and stopped at the rear of the Skylark, on her side.

"Oh, flat tire," he said. "I was worried it was . . ." He thrust his chin toward the GMC house. "Anyway, can I help you with that, ma'am?"

"Thank you, sir." Bond said. "I got it."

"You look stout enough to handle the lugs. Want me to hold my flashlight on it while you work?"

"Sure," she said. She hurriedly rubbed her cheek clean with her sleeve.

He laid his gun on the ground and walked to her. She jacked the tire off the ground and broke the lugs with ease.

"You want a job on my ranch?" he said.

She pulled the tire off and threw it to the side.

"I did ranch work when I was a girl. Got about enough of it." She looked up at him with a half smile. "But thanks."

He shined his light on the slashed tire. "What's this about?"

Bond stood, rolled the spare to the wheel, and slid it on the bolts. "Must of run over a hay hook fell off a truck."

"Mmm," he said without conviction.

She hand-tightened all the lug nuts and finished them with the lug wrench. There was no hubcap. She flipped the jack switch and palmed the bobbing jack handle as the tire took the car's weight.

The rancher said, "I haven't seen anyone handle a bumper jack in twenty years."

Bond put the Maglite in her pocket, picked up the slashed tire in one hand, the jack and wrench in the other, and walked to the trunk. She stood on the driver's side to block the rancher's view of the glass shards in his driveway. When she had stowed everything and shut the lid, she turned to him as he was picking up his shotgun. "Thank you, sir." She waited as he put the gun in the crook of his left arm. "I don't like to hold a Maglite in my teeth."

"*Sir*," he said. "You say that like a cop."

"I was raised to say it," she said. "Good night."

He nodded. "Night." His light bounced down the driveway. As Bond turned, he shouted, "Hey!"

She pointed her flashlight at him. He was facing her. "That house over there?" He pointed toward the crooks' place.

She looked toward it and then back at the rancher. "Yeah?" she shouted.

"That place is trouble. You're lucky they didn't see you. Drive out the other way."

"I will. Thanks." She waved, and he turned back down the drive.

Bond collected the biggest pieces of broken glass, opened her door, and laid them gently on the passenger floorboard. She found the bumper, wedged it into the back seat, and started the car. Knowing the rancher would be watching her lights, she drove north, away from the house.

She didn't stop until she reached home. She pinched the window glass into a paper Sooner Foods grocery sack and dropped it on top of the bones in her trash.

CHAPTER 12

Maytubby's phone woke him. Forgetting his ribs, he tried to sit up. The pain forced him back down for a few seconds. On the second try, he got upright and looked at the glowing screen. It said "Jake" and "4:51 a.m." The room was faintly lit by a streetlamp.

"Should I have brought the freedman's Springfield?" Jill mumbled.

Maytubby turned his head over his shoulder, then shifted his body stiffly toward her. "Hey."

"Hey, yourself. Better get that."

"It's Jake Renaldo," he said. He picked up the phone and detached the charger wire. "Trooper Renaldo." He cleared his throat.

"Looks like you nailed it, Bill. Got a call from the Kingston Police in Marshall County."

"I know where it is, Jake." Maytubby attempted a chuckle and got a stitch in his side.

Renaldo laughed. "Anyway, pharmacy alarm went off there at one twenty. The patrol officer was at a domestic. When she got to the pharmacy, the place was a mess. I made it a little before two. GMC guys or whoever, they smashed a glass door and trashed the place. Won't know what they took until the pharmacist takes stock. They also ripped out the security cameras and smashed those and the computer that likely housed the video."

"If it was the GMC guys, I found their place. Chadwick Road. I'll send you a satellite photo. They may not go home, but you can tell Scrooby and Murray County."

"Thanks, Bill. Will do," Renaldo said.

Maytubby found the satellite photo and texted it to Jake. He slid the phone into his uniform pants pocket and lay back on the bed.

Jill rolled toward him and felt his forehead. "No fever, at least," she said.

He breathed in the scent of her French soap. Ginger. It was one of their indulgences.

She lay against his side but kept her right hand on his shoulder. "Your shoulder loop is stiff, Sergeant."

"Is it, now?"

She rubbed his thigh. "Is it a harbinger?"

"Might be," he said. He rolled onto his right side and kissed her neck. His pain ebbed. Jill was wearing a navy cotton sleep shirt. She unbuttoned his uniform shirt and raised her arms while he pulled the shirt over her head. He kissed her breasts as she undid his trousers and pushed them off with her foot. He pulled her on top of him. She clinched his uniform shirt in her fists but kept her elbows off his ribs as she rocked gently, then avidly. His elbow knocked Emily Dickinson off the nightstand.

When they were spent, she rested her forehead in the hollow of his neck and ran her hands through his thick black hair. They panted, then settled. Her breath was sweet. Falling pecans popped on his roof. A rooster crowed in a neighbor's backyard.

Jill whispered in his ear, "You're absolutely no fun."

"Told you," he said.

He drew her to his chest and held the back of her neck. They kissed, gently at first, then hungrily.

She drew her face away, gripped his shoulders, and arched her back. She knitted her brow, flexed her thighs, and thrust with purpose.

The iron headboard thumped the wall. Maytubby flattened his right hand against her abdomen, murmured as he felt her muscles surge. He slid his thumb under her mons and let it rest in her slippery warmth. She bore down on his hand, let go of his shirt, and struck his shoulders with her fists as she cried out and shuddered. She fell on him and began to sob.

He stroked her back. This was something new. He remained quiet while she wept, quaking in his arms. He felt her hot tears on his neck.

Her breathing slowed, and she sniffed. She rubbed her nose on his shoulder loop and sat up, smiling.

"You okay?" he said, wiping her cheeks.

"Oh, yeah." She shook out her hair and peered at the night table. "We knocked Emily off her perch."

"I think her immortality is assured."

Jill swept a lock of his hair from his face. "I brought breakfast."

He drew her face down and kissed her.

When their faces were still close, she whispered, "And not nuts and berries."

"We haven't sunk to meat."

"I detect a note of yearning," she said.

"You detect right."

Jill pulled her sleep shirt from under a pillow and stood beside the bed. "You'll find out." She walked out of the bedroom, toward the kitchen.

Maytubby studied her hair as it swung over her back. He shucked off his uniform shirt, gathered his pants, and hung them both in his closet. He dressed in jeans and a well-worn long-sleeve shirt, gingerly slid a trail runner on his left foot, and laced it before he jammed on the right shoe.

When he walked into the kitchen, his Mr. Coffee sputtered into the carafe. It was still dark outside. The room was lit by a single bulb hanging from long braided wires. Jill was at the stove, wearing her Chickasaw Nation work clothes: an olive pantsuit, its blazer draped over a chair, a cranberry blouse, brown loafers, and the despised regulation pantyhose. She had tied the strings of his black apron in the back. He smelled frying meat.

Maytubby poured coffee into two Frankoma mugs shaped like oil drill bits. He carried one around Jill's back and set it beside the skillet. There were two flour tortillas on a plate beside the stove.

With her spatula, she pointed at red and green bell peppers and green onions on a wooden cutting board. "*Allez-y.*"

"*D'accord.*" Maytubby drank some coffee, took a wooden-handled chef's knife from the drawer below, and began mincing.

"That's the only French word you know, isn't it?"

He worked on the red pepper. "It is not. *Alors.* I know *alors.* I have it on good authority those are the only two words you need to get by in France."

Jill flipped the sausage in the iron skillet. "Oh, yeah? What authority is that?"

"I think it was Voltaire. Or maybe Mark Twain."

Jill blew a raspberry. "Wasn't it Mark Twain who learned how to say, 'Can you give me the directions to Jacksonville?' in several European languages?"

Maytubby moved on to the green pepper. "Mmmmm," he crooned. "It might have been."

"Faker," she said. She scooped up the sausage patties and dropped them onto a paper towel in a white saucer. She turned down the gas and cracked three eggs into a glass bowl.

Maytubby said, "What was your French teacher like at NYU?"

"Who said anything about NYU? I took four years of French at Ada High with Madame Corbin."

Maytubby stared at the peppers. Then he brightened. "Oh, yeah. I remember . . ." He pinched his nose and went on. "Madame *Cohr-bahn.*" He let go of his nose. "Tall lady with a bun."

"I bet you were one of those boys who made fun of her." Jill narrowed her eyes.

"Frog Lady, we called her. We stood up stiff, looked down our noses at each other, and spoke cartoon French gibberish. It was great fun."

Maytubby frowned and tapped the handle of his knife on the counter. "Also, a good way to pause being an Indian."

Jill turned off the fire. She gave him a serious look. "You ridiculed the outsider so you'd be less of an outsider."

"Not the first time, either," he said. "Or the last."

"I did that, too. Not with her." She wiped her hands on the apron. "Madame Corbin didn't notice ethnic differences—or didn't seem to. She treated all her students equally—with the same intolerance of bad pronunciation and grammar. Did you know she was from Camargue, that swampy wild part of southern France? She was a poor girl who married an Oklahoma oil patch guy on vacation. He brought her to Oklahoma City and divorced her. She went to OU, got a degree in French, and ended up here."

"A triple outsider—in France, in Oklahoma City, and in Ada." Maytubby leaned on the counter. "Have you seen her since you got back from New York?"

Jill relit the stove. "No. She died before she could retire. After I passed the ACTFL French test in New York, I sent her an email to thank her. Too late."

"*Alors*," he said.

Jill frowned and nodded. "*Alors.*"

She stirred the eggs with a fork.

Maytubby said, "What kind of sausage?"

"Venison. No pork in there, either. Just olive oil. Friend from work shot a buck near that buffalo ranch in Wanette." She salted and peppered the eggs and stirred them gently.

With the knife, Maytubby slid the peppers and onions off the board into the skillet. They hissed. "Should I be jealous?" He crumbled some Manchego cheese into a bowl.

"Probably. She's tall and handsome. And shoots an old Winchester lever-action with no scope."

"Now you're just preying on my male insecurities."

Jill stirred the peppers and onions. "Also, she's pretty much always fun."

She poured the eggs into two pools, one larger than the other. Then she slid the peppers and onions onto each. Maytubby lifted the bowl of Manchego and sprinkled crumbs onto the eggs. He limped to the table and laid silverware and cotton napkins while she finished the omelets and pressed tortillas on the skillet.

They filled their plates at the stove and carried them and the coffee mugs to the table. The neighbor's rooster crowed again. They ate greedily, without speaking.

When they had wiped their plates with folded tortillas and finished those, they took up their coffee mugs and fell back in their chairs.

"You studied French at St. John's," Jill said.

"*Oui m'dame. Mais je ne parle pas couramment.*"

"I'm not fluent either." She hugged her drill bit and sipped coffee. "But look at us. Our own native speakers are dwindling, and we chased the fancy tongues."

"Hannah Bond knows more Chickasaw than I do," Maytubby said. "She's been taking Chickasaw at the nation's night school for years."

Jill said, "We hankered for the wide, wide world."

Maytubby nodded and drank from his mug. "At least we're both doing *Chikashshanompa* Rosetta Stone on our laptops."

She smiled. "You skip all the first lessons?"

"I did," Maytubby said. "Our grandparents taught us a few words."

Maytubby carried their plates and utensils to the sink, washed them, and set them in a drainer. While he scoured the skillet with salt, he said, "Where do you take the anti-sugar crusade today?"

"Tupelo Elementary."

"We may cross paths. Hannah and I are taking our days off to go to—"

"Cairo," Jill said. "I remember. You're looking for Cy Mead's family." She sipped her coffee.

"Since we don't have an ID on the body, I decided to talk to my great-aunt Maytubby, who lives near them. Maybe she knows something."

"I saw the bruises on your side," Jill said. "Must hurt, bending over to change your foot dressing. Want me to help?"

"I need to make it hurt to stretch it out," Maytubby said. "Not to mention that your pantsuit would incite animal lust."

"That'd be a first." She stood and donned her jacket. "I'm off to the nation parking lot to pick up the van."

"Filled with plaster broccoli and tomatoes."

"But no sausage," Jill said.

"*Chokma*," he said. Good. They kissed. "*Yakoke*." Thank you.

CHAPTER 13

Before Maytubby left his house, he tossed two old open-reel fishing poles into his pickup bed. Their fraying cotton line dangled red-and-white plastic bobbers, lead sinkers, and rusted hooks. When he pulled into Hannah's yard at seven, the Skylark was missing. He knocked on her door and waited. When he turned around, Hannah was walking into the yard under the sodium streetlight, a Band-Aid on her bruised cheek.

"Hey, Bill," she said. "Looks like we'll be takin' your pickup." She opened the front door of her house and led him in. She still wore the flannel shirt and jeans. "I'll get us some coffee. It's still warm."

Maytubby sat at her table. The room smelled of bacon and bananas. Hannah didn't eat bananas, so he knew he was smelling Hoppe's No. 9 bore solvent. Bond had been cleaning her Model 10.

Hannah settled mugs on the table and sat. "Just left the Buick at Garn's for bodywork and a new used tire. I was spyin' on our Chadwick Road friends. 'Bout midnight they came out on the porch. Must of seen the Buick before they got in the GMC. I was going to follow 'em, but they backed all the way to where I was. Fast and fishtailin'. Caught me by surprise."

Maytubby sipped his coffee. "They thought you were law?"

Hannah snorted. "They thought I was teenagers fuckin' in the country. Princess threw a big rock through my window." She pointed at her cheek. "Poor thang. I ruint his fun. Red slashed my tire before he learnt of their failed mission." She smiled wanly and took a long draw of coffee. "Nice rancher fella helped me change the tire. He suspected the maggots. I told him I run over a hay hook."

Maytubby nodded. "Jake Renaldo called me around five this morning. Break-in at a Kingston pharmacy at one twenty. Deputy was out on a call. Camera record destroyed."

"Figures," Hannah said.

"I gave Jake the Chadwick Road address."

Hannah drained her coffee and frowned. "We best get going," she said. "You got your nuts and berries?"

Maytubby took their mugs to the sink. "I do."

Hannah grabbed a paper sack from the table and lifted the 89er baseball cap and her duty belt from a peg by the door, grabbed her Steiners from a stool. She held up the sack. "Slim Jims and jerky. Where's your camo hat?"

"Different hat," he said. "Stonewall Longhorns. In the truck."

"Got it. Red saw the camo. Throw him off the scent." Hannah twisted her lips. "If he plumb forgot your pickup." She paused before she opened the cab door. "I never known you to fish." She pointed at the rods.

Maytubby shrugged. "We'll be tooling around lakes and creeks. Never hurts to have an alibi."

When they crossed the Blue, Maytubby and Bond flipped down their sun visors and pulled down the bills of their caps against the sunrise. Hannah said, "Who is this great-aunt of yours we're goin' to visit?"

"She's my dad's father's sister. Never married. In her eighties now. Lives alone on a tiny piece of an old allotment. She worked in stores in Coalgate until she got Social Security. Raises a big garden, last I knew. Haven't seen her in many years."

"She a speaker?" Hannah said.

"She is."

"Want me to try some of my night school lingo?"

"Sure," Maytubby said.

As they neared Clarita, Maytubby braked for an Amish wagon crossing the highway.

"Damned if that isn't Aaron Coblentz," Hannah said, pointing to the driver. "Same buckskin gelding."

"Rings a bell," Maytubby said, to be polite. He recalled Hannah's Amishman perfectly.

"I talked to him around Bromide—he was in his buggy—after the Majesty Tate murder. He called me from his barn phone after he saw that bastard Hillers riding away from the Tate house on his mountain bike."

"Striking blue eyes, you said."

"That guy," Hannah said. They crossed the Clear Boggy. Cottonwoods flashed golden in the early sun.

"Last spring," Hannah said, "when we were explaining the Verner killing to Scrooby, you told him you learned Greek in college."

"Ancient Greek, yeah. And French. They were required." Maytubby didn't want to get ahead of her.

But Hannah said nothing.

"You're wondering about my Chickasaw," Maytubby said.

"None of my business," she said.

"I have snatches from my *ippo'si'*."

"Your grandma," Hannah said.

Maytubby nodded. "When I was young it didn't seem important. My dad thought it was useless."

"Old-timey," Hannah said.

"Yeah," Maytubby said. He bumped his left hand on the steering wheel. "And when I went to college in Santa Fe, I was all in for the prestige languages."

Hannah nodded.

"You know, I haven't been going to night school with you, because I'm embarrassed," Maytubby said.

"None of my affairs," she said.

"Jill and I have been studying Chickasaw on the sly. A computer platform called Rosetta Stone." He glanced at his rearview. "Wait, what's this?"

Two vehicles whipped around the Ford.

"First one looks like the maggots' GMC," Hannah said. "Who's chasin' 'em?"

Maytubby accelerated, watched the red needle on his dial speedometer lean to 110 and pause. The vehicle tailing the GMC was a seventies-vintage Barracuda, a muscle car. Purple. As Maytubby closed the tail, Hannah got busy searching the Barracuda's plate on her phone's police app.

The Barracuda's single working brake light flashed, and the GMC fishtailed onto a dirt road. The 'Cuda's brakes locked. Maytubby's did, too. Rubber smoke rose from the screeching tires. The Barracuda slewed, narrowly missed the bar ditch, and spun up dust as it pursued the GMC. Maytubby slowed and continued up the highway, watching the dust plume move north. "Damn stolen plate again," Hannah said.

Maytubby steered onto the grass shoulder, made a U-turn, and returned to the dirt road. "From where?"

"Coalgate," she said. "Playin' with fire in his own backyard."

The Ford shuddered on the washboard road as Maytubby accelerated toward the plume. A stray dog froze in the ditch and eyed the truck. At the top of a rise, they saw the plume drift away from the road, revealing both stopped vehicles, at odd angles to one another. Maytubby braked hard and pulled onto a driveway apron. The Barracuda had apparently got ahead of the GMC and cut it off.

As Hannah dug out her Steiners, she said, "*This* ought to be a rodeo."

Maytubby watched Hannah's face. She said, "Everbody's out of their vehicles, two guys from the 'Cuda and Red and Princess. The 'Cuda guys shouldering long guns. Assault kind. They're wearing black bandannas over their faces, black ball caps. Looks like they got the drop on the maggots. Maggots dropping their pistols, putting their hands on the truck hood. Uhhh, one masked guy is picking up the pistols." She burst out laughing.

"What?" Maytubby said.

"The 'Cuda guys are both short. The one not picking up the pistols tried to jump into the GMC bed. His gunstock hit him in the nuts, and he fell back on the ground. Bendin' over . . . Now he's givin' it another go while his partner is sticking the pistols in his pants. What a bunch a goobers."

Maytubby watched the road behind him in the rearview.

"Okay," Hannah said, "He made it this time. Lessee, he's got a big black garbage bag full of somethin', throwin' it onto the road. He tossed his rifle down after it. Learnt his lesson. He's back on the ground, got his rifle and the bag, toting the bag to the 'Cuda. Unlocking the trunk, in goes the bag . . . the other guy backs toward the 'Cuda." She hummed to herself a few seconds. "Now!" she said and lowered her Steiners.

Maytubby pulled out of the drive and gave chase to the Barracuda.

Hannah said, "Slow down a little at the Jimmy so I can take a picture."

As he passed the GMC, Princess and Red were turning and separating to mount the cab. Hannah's camera pattered with burst shots. When they had passed the GMC, she said, "Hee *hee*. Them 'Cuda guys were too dumb to take their keys."

Maytubby accelerated for a few seconds, slowed to let his own dust settle, then sped up to keep ahead of the GMC. Hannah raised her Steiners. The Barracuda section-lined west by north, slewing at every ninety-degree turn. The tail was easy as long as the muscle car was on dirt roads. In his mirror, he could see the GMC's plume, far behind.

"Out goes one pistol," Hannah said. "Not total idjits. Except their prints'll be all over." She set the binoculars in her lap. When Maytubby neared the spot, Hannah said "Riiiiight *there*." Both of them looked out his window at a stand of red sumac, which receded fast. Hannah said, "What about the other'n'?"

"Maybe they liked it," Maytubby said.

Near Tupelo, the Barracuda's dust cloud settled. Hannah raised her Steiners. "They're turnin' back east toward Coalgate, on the highway," she said. Maytubby hit his brakes and made a right on Stonecipher Road. At the highway intersection, he waited until the Barracuda roared by. He floored the gas pedal. "Might be out of our league," he said as the Ford bucked onto asphalt.

"In a pig's eye, Bill. This V-eight is big as a hay bale."

The Barracuda slalomed around farm trucks and tractors. Maytubby followed suit, hanging a half mile back. He disliked high-speed pursuits—too much collateral damage—but in this case the target wasn't fleeing him. He scanned the intersections ahead. In his mirror, the GMC was a speck.

Hannah calmly peeled a Slim Jim and munched on it. Speed didn't faze her.

The purple car's one brake light flashed an instant before tire smoke veiled it. The Barracuda turned north. It slowed now. Maytubby slowed as well. When he reached the intersection, he saw the road sign for Coalgate Reservoir and turned. A rusted yellow sign said Dead End. The road curved into dense post oaks. Driveways led to well-tended mobile homes back in the trees.

Hannah said, "Think the GMC saw us turn?" She polished off her Slim Jim and stuffed the wrapper into her paper bag.

"I don't think so," Maytubby said. He checked his rearview. No dust, no pickup.

There were no more driveways, and the road split. The left fork shrank to a pair of ruts. Maytubby went left. He downshifted and listened to the grass between the ruts brush the Ford's undercarriage. "Hannah, snap a picture on your phone and drop a pin in Google Maps."

Maytubby braked the pickup to a stop, shifted into first. "I didn't pack my goober teeth."

She raised her eyebrows. "So we're goin' in. Who am I in this deal?"

"I was thinking my wife."

"Better park far back," Hannah said. She pulled the bill of her cap down over her eyes.

Maytubby mussed his hair, scraped some down over his forehead, and pulled the Stonewall Longhorns cap down low. He let the Ford idle for five minutes, checking his mirror as they waited. Then he let out the clutch and followed the winding ruts for a quarter mile. The Barracuda appeared, facing toward him, its trunk open. It was backed up to a ruined, unpainted shed. Its front door was open, and an open padlock dangled from a hasp. The rock foundation of a long-gone house squatted to his left, beside it a rusted water pump.

The front plate on the muscle car read ASK ME ABOUT MY GRAND-KIDS. There was no one in sight when Maytubby killed his engine and got out of the Ford. He stood for a few seconds before he shouted, "Hey! Anybody home?"

Two short men bolted out of the shack. They were unarmed. They wore the black hats but had their bandannas pulled down over their throats. They halted and stared at Maytubby, then threw glances at the Barracuda.

"Hey, there! Me and my wife . . ." He threw out his arm toward the Ford. "We was tryin' to get to this lake for some catfishin'." He pointed in the direction of the reservoir. "We seen the sign on the paved road."

Maytubby glanced back and forth between the faces and realized the men were identical twins. Same blunt nose, same full lips. They frowned but relaxed. In unison, they pointed back up the track. In unison, they said, "Go back up to the fork." The one on the left looked at his brother, who said, "Take a right there."

Maytubby waved, nodding vigorously. "Thanks s'much!" He walked slowly back to the Ford, got in, started the engine, and shifted into reverse.

As he stretched his arm across the back seat behind Hannah and turned his head to back up the trail, she said, "You never even proposed." The truck groaned and shuddered on the sand. "I put my phone down to the dash, zoomed in and took their picture."

"Twins," he said.

The pickup gained the fork. Maytubby shifted into first and headed back to the highway.

Hannah yanked another Slim Jim out of her sack and began to peel it. "We can find the gun easy," she said.

They reached the sumac stand without sighting the GMC. Maytubby parked the Ford. Hannah unsnapped a pouch in her duty belt, pulled on a pair of nitrile gloves. She dumped Slim Jims from her paper sack onto the floorboard, then emptied Maytubby's snacks beside them.

"Hey!" Maytubby said.

"One for the pistol, one for the bullets," Hannah said.

Maytubby frowned, took out his camera, and photographed the road. Then he dropped a pin and sent the map to himself. He and Hannah got out of the truck and waded into the sumac.

Shortly, they walked up from the ditch, Hannah carrying a pistol.

"What you got?" Maytubby said.

"Kimber forty-five."

OSBI did not accept loaded guns at evidence intake. Bond ejected a chambered round and the magazine. Unfired cartridges were useless to ballistics, but they might carry DNA or a print from the person who loaded them.

They climbed into the cab. Hannah slipped the gun and cartridges into two separate sacks and snapped off her gloves.

CHAPTER 14

The Cairo, Oklahoma, post office was shuttered in 1939. The place still appeared on maps, a dot on State Highway 131. Maytubby turned south from the highway on Hooe Road and drove slowly until the road petered out in the big bur oaks shading Coal Creek. He stopped and considered several branched tracks. Then he took the leftmost. His great-aunt's native stone cottage, roofed with tin sheets, sat on the bank of the creek.

Maytubby parked the Ford next to his great-aunt's old Honda, took off his hat, and combed his hair with his fingers. He grubbed some pecans off the floorboard and tossed them in his mouth. Hannah also removed her cap.

He got out of the pickup and stood silent. He could hear the stream, and a crow croaking up in the trees. In a few minutes, the front door opened, and a woman with long gray hair appeared. She wore a long, loose cotton dress, navy with orange embroidery. She was holding a long wooden spoon.

"*Chipisalika chokma, Sashko'si' ishto* Lydia," he said.

Hannah looked at him and widened her eyes a smidge.

Lydia reached into a loose pocket in her dress, took out a pair of glasses, unfolded them, and slipped them on. She walked a few paces closer, stopped, and then smiled. "*Chokma*, William. I haven't seen you since your *inki'* died." She threw a glance at Hannah.

Maytubby gestured for Hannah to join them. As she was getting out of the pickup, Maytubby said, "This is my friend, Deputy Bond." Hannah walked to Maytubby's side.

Lydia Maytubby said to her grand-nephew, "Yes, yes. You're the Lighthorseman."

"Hannah, this is my great-aunt Lydia Maytubby."

To Lydia, Hannah said, "*Chokma. Saholhchifoat* Hannah. *Chin Chokma ta?*"

Lydia said, "*Achokma akinni,*" and smiled at Hannah.

Lydia looked at Maytubby and then threw her eyes toward Hannah. "*Chickashshaw* Bond?"

Maytubby smiled and shook his head. "Not that she knows."

Lydia waved her spoon and said, "Come inside. You're in luck. I'm making *pashofa*. Almost done. It's a big pot for church potluck. Plenty for you."

Maytubby and Hannah followed her in. She walked to her stove and stirred a large pot. The scent of stewing hominy and salt pork took Maytubby back to his grandmother's kitchen. His mother had died when he was four, and his father wasn't much of a cook.

"Sit at the table," Lydia said.

Maytubby and Hannah sat in wooden chairs with caned seats, at a square pine table. There was a bud vase with a few sprigs of rosemary at the center. Lydia stirred the stew. The small room had a softwood floor and pine paneling. There were braided cotton rugs on the floor, and a large rock hearth with a cook-pot swing arm.

Lydia filled crockery bowls with a wooden ladle and carried them to the table. As they steamed, she filled jelly glasses with tap water and brought them and some spoons to set beside the bowls. She took a seat at the table and picked up her spoon. She nodded, waited for her guests to begin eating before she did. Maytubby and Hannah blew on the stew in their spoons to cool it.

After Hannah had taken a bite, she said, "This is good groceries, Lydia."

Lydia was tickled by the expression.

"Yes. And good memories," Maytubby said.

They ate quietly. A few bur oak acorns, big as golf balls, banged on the roof.

When they had finished, Maytubby picked up the bowl and spoons, carried them to the sink, washed them, and set them in the drainer. "Which is the hand towel?" he said to Lydia.

She smiled archly at Hannah. "Which towel."

To Maytubby she said, "There's only one towel, William."

He dried his hands on a tea towel hanging over the oven handle and took his seat at the table.

"You always were helpful to your *ippo'si'*," Lydia said. She looked at her guests. "Now, since I have two police officers visiting my house, you must be here on business."

Maytubby pursed his lips and nodded. "I'm sorry, but yes."

"I am happy to help if I can, William."

"Do you know a *Chickashsha* family near here named Mead?" Maytubby said.

"Oh, yes. They live five miles north, a little east. I've known them for years." She frowned. "Is something wrong?"

"We don't know." Maytubby stared at the table and then over Lydia's head. "Is there a young man in the family named Cy?"

Lydia stuck out her lower lip and lowered her brow. "Cy couldn't be in trouble with the law. He's the sweetest kid in the world. Wins prizes with his rabbits and sheep in 4-H. Drives his *ippo'si'* over here so we can have Bible study and coffee. The three of us go to Johnson Chapel every other Sunday."

"He's not in trouble with the law," Maytubby said, and then quickly continued. "Did Cy ever mention anything about an old family allotment around Mill Creek, in Johnston County?"

Lydia rolled her eyes. "Lord, yes. His mother told me he couldn't stop talking about it. Bee in his bonnet. Some uncle mentioned it to him at Festival a year ago. Cy even drove over to the courthouse in Tishomingo to look in the old Dawes Indian books." She flattened her hands on the table, half-smiled, and swiveled her eyes between Maytubby and Hannah. "Gotten to be kind of a family joke. Pipe dream, you know. Most of those first allotments were sold off long ago." She waved her hand dismissively.

Maytubby considered reminding his aunt that the house she lived in—lent to her in perpetuity by a late friend—was built on a Choctaw allotment that had never been sold. But he let that pass. His great-aunt had answered his question. What should he tell her now? He shuffled his memories. Lydia was not a gossip. One of the kin his father and grandmother trusted.

"William?" Lydia said.

"Aunt Lydia, Cy's family reported him missing four days ago."

Lydia covered her mouth with her right hand and said softly, "No." She shook her head. She removed her hand. "Do you"—she looked at Hannah—"and Deputy Hannah know what . . . where he is?"

Hannah looked at Maytubby, poker-faced.

"We don't know anything for certain. I think it would be best if we all wait to speak with the Meads until we do."

Lydia dropped her hand on the table and nodded slowly. "I understand, William. You and Deputy Hannah are investigating."

Maytubby almost said, "And others," but stopped himself from lying. "Yes. *Yakoke*, Aunt Lydia. Can you tell me exactly where Cy lives and what kind of car he drives?"

She gave him precise directions, on the plains' cardinal grid. Five miles north, one mile east, a half mile north. "The car is a red Ford." Lydia knitted her brow. "It only has two doors, 'cause it's hard for me to get in the back. It's small, not new. The back comes up. What d'y'call it?"

"A hatchback," Maytubby said. "Hold on." He pulled out his phone, found a picture of a red 2001 Focus, and showed it to her. To Hannah he said, "Two thousand one Ford Focus hatchback."

Lydia adjusted her glasses and peered at his phone. "That's it," she said.

Maytubby pocketed his phone. "You have given us important information."

She nodded soberly and said, "*Chokma.*" Good. She rose quickly and walked to her refrigerator. From it, she carried a pie tin to the counter. She turned to Maytubby and Bond. "You have work to do. I'm sending some pecan pie with you. The little natives from my trees." She cut two slices and wrapped them individually in waxed paper.

Hannah said, "Those little boogers are hard to pick out. But they're the sweetest."

Lydia carried the pie to the table and handed one to each of her guests. "I always thought so."

Maytubby and Hannah rose. Maytubby hugged his aunt. As he stepped back, she patted his chest and said, "Why aren't you and Deputy Hannah wearing your uniforms?" She gestured toward her front yard. "And why are you driving your dad's old pickup instead of a Lighthorse car?"

Maytubby grinned at her and narrowed his eyes.

After a pause, she said, "Ohhh. So the neighbors wouldn't think old Lydia robbed a bank."

He nodded and smiled.

"*Chipisala'cho!*" he said as he waved goodbye from the door. Hannah repeated the farewell.

Lydia watched them from her door as they drove away.

Hannah unwrapped her slice of pie, ate it in three bites, balled up the waxed paper, and tossed it on the floorboard. "Where to now, Sergeant William? I mean, after the Mead house."

"To a liquor store in Coalgate."

CHAPTER 15

"I figgered you had secret vices," Hannah said as they drove past Angus ranches and hayfields on the way to the Meads'.

Maytubby blushed. Hannah wasn't looking at him.

"The liquor store owner has helped me with cases. She's Jake Renaldo's second cousin."

"A Eye-talian, like him? From the coal miners back in the day?"

"Yeah. Her store is across the street from a beat-up rent house our crooks are drawn to."

"Like who?" Hannah said.

"Old Steel-Toe from the Verner murder and the fellow burnt up in Antlers, Wiley Bates."

"Maybe we should find the landlord."

Maytubby took the last section line left and slowed. "Maybe we shouldn't. Kill the golden goose."

"I take your point. There's the Mead place." Hannah pointed.

Maytubby stopped just before they reached the little frame house. He photographed it and dropped a pin in Maps. As they rolled past the house, Hannah said, "We don't expect the Focus to be there."

Maytubby accelerated. "No. Surely the Coal County sheriff is looking for it." He made the next left and drove toward Coalgate.

"Or not," Hannah said. "Or maybe it's in Johnston County." She pulled out her phone. "I'm callin' Garn. I paid him to get LeeRoy out of the ditch . . ."

"Hannah."

She shook her head dismissively. "Maybe somebody paid him to get the Focus out of their ditch. 'Cause it was a eyesore."

"You're right," Maytubby said.

Hannah held the phone to her ear. "Hey, Garn, it's Hannah." Maytubby heard him talking. "No, Garn," she said, "I'm not calling about the Buick. I don't expect it to be done yet. Listen, have you towed an old red Ford Focus out of somebody's ditch in the last few days?" Maytubby heard Garn talking. Hannah nodded. "Yeah . . . Yeah. So can you tell me just where the car was?" She nodded some more and glanced at Maytubby. "Got it," she said into the phone. "Any damage?" Hannah listened. "And you towed it to your garage?" Garn talked at some length. Hannah rolled her eyes. Then she interrupted him. "Thanks, Garn. I'll be over to have a look. Don't let anybody touch that Focus. No hurry with the Buick. *Bye.*"

Hannah put her phone away. "Man," she said. "He must get lonely workin' on cars."

"Where'd he tow it from?"

"Rock Creek low-water crossing on Rocky Road, the one south of Mill Creek, by Ten-Acre Rock. It was blocking traffic. Some water over the floorboard. Facing east, damage high up on the right rear."

Maytubby said, "So Mead was fleeing Princess and Red on a back road . . ."

"One he didn't know and they did. 'Stead of taking the highway straight back to Coalgate and Cairo."

Maytubby passed a tractor. "I don't remember any houses by that crossing on Rock Creek. There's an abandoned rock house a quarter mile east."

Hannah said, "You're the one with the road mem'ry in his head."

At the Coalgate city limits, asphalt pavement gave way to bricks on Main Street. The pickup rumbled. They passed some tidy Section

8 housing and a faded mural on the side of a tall brick Victorian building—a rodeo bull throwing its rider. Maytubby remembered that the
town's first worked coal seam ran right down Main, on the surface
of the earth.

Just before they pulled into the graveled liquor store parking lot,
Maytubby pointed to the crooks' house across the street. A hand-
lettered FOR RENT sign with a phone number was stapled to a stake.

"Now's our chance," Hannah said.

Maytubby parked in the lot. It was still early in the afternoon,
but two other pickups and a new sedan were already in the lot. He
and Hannah got out of the truck. She waited for him to take the lead.
Through the store's large glass pane, he could see Lorenza Mercante
ringing up and sacking bottles. Her patrons twisted the sack tops before
lifting their purchases from the counter. Maytubby stopped short of the
three wooden stairs leading up to the entrance. Hannah stood beside
him. Customers on their way out filed past them. When the store had
emptied, Maytubby opened the door and held it for Hannah.

He watched Lorenza Mercante's face as Hannah entered. Her
eyes lifted to Bond's face, her mouth forming a polite, closed smile.
When Maytubby stepped from behind Hannah, trying not to limp,
Lorenza blinked and then smiled broadly. She walked to the edge of
the counter and, as he feared, opened her hands and lifted her long,
dark hair over her head and let it fall over her shoulders. He blushed.

"Well, hey, Lighthorseman! Where's your plane? Last time, you
parked it on the strip and walked in my back door." She looked at
Hannah and stuck her hands in her jeans pockets. "He caught me cutting boxes of Mad Dog." She lowered her face and squinted up at
Hannah. "Too polite to call me on it."

Maytubby half relaxed. Lorenza Mercante had lifted a finger to
the wind.

He said, "Ms. Mercante . . ." and waited a beat for her usual
demand that he call her Lorenza. It didn't come. "This is Deputy
Hannah Bond, from Johnston County."

Lorenza appeared pleased by this news. She stepped forward

and shook Hannah's hand. "Nice to meet you, Deputy Bond. Lorenza Mercante."

Hannah said, "Manners he's got. Thanks for your help on our cases. Sergeant Maytubby tells me that house across the road has been a hideout."

The shop door opened. Bond and Maytubby nodded to the owner and shuffled aside to inspect her stock. The customer, a graying man in a blue suit and red tie, walked directly to the Scotch shelf, pulled off a bottle of Glenfiddich, and set it gently on the counter. Lorenza checked him out. He twisted the paper bag top and left the store.

Maytubby and Bond walked back to the counter. Maytubby said, "Was that Judge Lalala?"

Lorenza Mercante laughed. "You remembered! He's on recess." She looked out the front window. "I wonder why everybody twists the top of their sacks."

Hannah said, "So folks won't see the tops of their bottles and know they're buying hooch."

"A dead giveaway, then," Lorenza said.

"Yes, ma'am."

Lorenza smiled and crossed her arms. "I know you guys have questions and pictures. Shoot."

Maytubby said, "Deputy Bond—"

"Hannah," Lorenza said. She looked at Bond and said, "I know. He always tries to call me 'Ms. Mercante.'"

"Hannah," Maytubby said, "has some pictures on her phone. We'd like to know if you recognize vehicles or people."

Bond pulled out her phone. Lorenza moved closer to her. "First the black GMC pickup," Bond said, using two fingers to enlarge the photo of Princess and Red. "Common around here." Lorenza nodded. Bond swiped. "Then these two jokers." She again enlarged the photo.

Lorenza bent closer to the phone and peered at the figures. She drew her head back and shook it. "No. Sorry," she said.

Bond swiped and then spread her fingers on a third photo. "This old purple 'Cuda."

Lorenza canted her head for only a second before she pointed at the screen and said, "Oh, yeah. And I know who's standing next to it. You don't even have to zoom in. The O'Hara twins."

Maytubby began, "Could—"

"Larry and Jerry," Lorenza said. "They came in not long after I bought the store. Trailing clouds of body spray. One of 'em was writing me a check for Old Crow while the other was trying to stick a bottle of"—she looked at Maytubby—"speakin' of, Mad Dog Twenty-Twenty into his jeans. I made him take it out, and I tore up the check. Eighty-sixed 'em both. Called the bank, and of course the check would have bounced."

Hannah and Maytubby waited.

Lorenza folded her arms and looked beyond them to the front window. "They blew into Coalgate a few years ago, from who knows where." She waved a hand. "Bought that purple muscle car from an old man who had owned it forever."

"Ask me about my grandkids," Hannah said.

Lorenza laughed and shook her head. "Yeah. As if somebody roarin' around in a purple hot rod could hide behind that. They've been in and out of county lockup from the git-go. Bar fights, speeding, discharging firearms in the city limits. They always get lawyers and bail, somehow. Nobody seems to know where they get the money."

Maytubby said, "Do you know—"

"They've moved around. I heard that right now they live in a trailer," Lorenza said, "Out on Old Sprague Road, north of Thirty-One about a half mile. Can't tell you what it looks like." She narrowed her eyes at the front window. "My guess is, they're worse than small-town hoodlums. They're known to cruise around in that 'Cuda and shoot stray dogs wandering the ditches. That's not illegal—sheep ranchers kill packs that go after their stock—but it's cruel." She sighed. A Hiland Dairy tanker downshifted on the highway.

Maytubby took three steps to a shelf with a small wine selection. He chose a Sonoma Zinfandel and set it on the counter. Lorenza raised her brows and unfolded her arms. As she walked behind the counter, he said, "Off duty."

She said, "What happened to your foot?"

"I stepped in a game trap at night." He took out his wallet and handed her two twenties.

She handed him the change and sacked his bottle. "Off duty then, too."

Hannah stood stock-still. She looked out the back window at the municipal airport runway.

"Yeah," he said softly.

She looked at him as she slid the sack toward him, briefly caught his eye. She nodded and smiled.

"Thank you for your help, Lorenza. Again." He picked up the sack.

Hannah said, "So you gonna twist the top, or what?"

Maytubby said, "No. I'll live dangerously." Before he turned, he said, "Could I have a couple extra sacks?"

She handed them to him. "For crime scene evidence?"

"If we're lucky." He cradled the bottle in his arm and followed Hannah toward the front door. Two pickups drove into the lot, both with cattle panels on the beds. Lorenza followed him closely. After Hannah opened the door, Lorenza laid a hand on his trapezius muscle and squeezed. He blushed and took the first step down.

CHAPTER 16

As Maytubby drove toward Old Sprague Road, Hannah stared out the windshield and said, "Why are you scairt of your spy back there?"

Maytubby was startled but not surprised. Lorenza had given nothing away, which excused Hannah from a charge of meddling. "Because she's an attractive woman and I've never mentioned her to Jill. And vice versa. You know I'm going to share that wine with Jill, but I didn't tell Lorenza that."

"Oh," Hannah said. She sat quietly for a few seconds and then smiled faintly. "Your spy is really good, then."

Maytubby also smiled faintly.

"I got to call Sheriff Magaw and tell him about the Focus. Wish I didn't." She swiped her phone, tapped it, and held it to her ear.

"Scrooby's going to ask Garn when you called him about it," Maytubby said.

Hannah nodded. "Hi, it's Hannah. Can I speak to Sheriff Magaw?" Maytubby turned onto Old Sprague Road. "Sheriff Magaw, Garn towed a red 2001 Ford Focus hatchback to his garage. It was reported abandoned, blocking the low-water crossing on Rocky Road. Damage high up on the right rear. It's so close to the Ten-Acre Rock, and that GMC ran LeeRoy Sickles off the road. You might want to make the Focus a crime scene and inform OSBI. I'm driving right now. Talk to you later." She pulled the phone away from her face. Maytubby could hear Magaw talking when she ended the call. Her phone vibrated a few seconds later. She ignored it. "There was no body damage on that 'Cuda. Besides, the damage to Mead's Focus was high up, Garn said."

They passed three mobile homes before the road ended in a T. No Barracuda. Maytubby made a U-turn and retraced his path. "Which one, you think? Not the one with toys in the yard."

"I'm bettin' on the one with no shrubs and the pile of beer cans around a dead campfire."

"Yeah," Maytubby said. They drove to it and stopped on the road. Maytubby took out his phone, photographed it, and dropped a mapping pin. The nearest home, mobile or otherwise, was a quarter mile away. "I don't see any cameras. Hope Larry or Jerry isn't home." They eyed the closed mini-blinds, which didn't stir.

Hannah pulled her cap over her eyes. "I'm gonna dig around in that fire ring right quick. You see anybody comin', honk." She bailed out of the cab, grabbed a stick with dried leaves on one end out of the ditch, and made it to the dead fire in ten long strides. Maytubby checked the road ahead, his rearview, and the trailer windows. He watched Hannah bend over and probe the ashes and burnt logs with the leafless end of her stick. She stood and surveyed the yard. Then she backed toward the pickup, scouring out her boot prints with the stick's leafy end.

When Hannah climbed back in the cab, her phone was vibrating. "I bet Benny Magaw is honked off." She smiled. "We can't spill the beans now."

"Until we have the whole can," Maytubby said, as he drove toward the highway. "What did you find?"

Hannah removed her cap and laid it in her lap. "No burnt billfold, dern it. Some big melted pill bottles and melted syringes with black needles."

"Larry and Jerry are cooking the Oxy and shooting it up."

Maytubby turned onto State 31. Hannah said, "Unless they got the sugar diabetes."

He laughed. "We may have better luck at Rocky Road."

"It hasn't rained, so maybe the creek hasn't carried our evidence too far," Hannah said.

"How do you think Larry and Jerry knew to ambush the GMC—or where it was?"

Hannah stared out the windshield, tapped her cap on her thigh. The highway unspooled between fence-line hedges of volunteer hackberries. "They'd know the competition, from maggot talk at country beer joints."

"Maybe even Princess and Red?"

Hannah scowled, shrugged.

When they neared Clarita, Maytubby braked for an Amish carriage. He checked his rearview and passed it slowly. "If Larry and Jerry had known about the stash at the crime scene, they would have raided it. Or tried to. That's the only way they'd have run into Mead."

Hannah said, "The boy would've had to get between them and the stash. But the Focus wasn't damaged by the 'Cuda. Maybe Mead got away from Princess and Red, made it back over Ten-Acre Rock to the property, and got caught by Larry and Jerry."

"Seems like a stretch," Maytubby said. "But never overestimate stumblebums."

"Does seem like a stretch. That low-ridin' 'Cuda would high-center on a horse turd. The trail up to their shed by Coalgate Reservoir was soft dirt and not rock like these."

"And the tool-forgers, the old hippie couple in Johnston County lockup. How could they not know about the stash in their own outbuilding?" Maytubby said. "Princess and Red must be holding something over them."

"Like knowing they were squatting. If the hippies didn't rat 'em out to Magaw or Scrooby, that must be it. They might claim they were renting the shack out for storage and had no idea what was in there."

A roadrunner darted across the highway. Maytubby said, "And

how would the, uh, artisans advertise their shed for rent? Put an ad on the Bumfuck Craigslist?"

"Maybe they just spread it around—country stores and gas stations."

"That would fit. They could put a Jackson to good use every month. Cigarettes or some Coleman gas. They might just ignore the creeps. They're hermits. But enterprising hermits. And I can't get over how they leave their blinds open at night and seem, I don't know, easy. Maybe they're not even trying to claim Indian land. Just found a beat-up house on unclaimed property."

Maytubby drove up onto the Big Rock prairie. Cattle grazed among jutting boulders. Wind towers appeared to the north, their white blades turning lazily.

"Long as the hippies been there," Hannah said, "they must've asked around or looked it up. You're turnin' soft on 'em, Bill."

Maytubby said, "Yeah. They're thieving from my people."

When they reached the descent to the Rocky Creek low-water crossing, Maytubby downshifted, found a small turnout above the stream, and braked to a stop. He turned off the engine.

"There's the ruts from the car and Garn's wrecker," Hannah said.

"Break off some of a Slim Jim for bait, and I'll get the rods and reels."

Hannah balked. "Who's gonna know if we baited our hooks?"

Maytubby said, "I threw a bunch of empty whiskey bottles back in the pickup bed to throw off meddlers—turned out Princess and Red. Paid off."

Hannah frowned and peeled a Slim Jim. Maytubby lifted the poles from the bed, and they baited the rusted hooks. Rocky Creek sprang from the Arbuckle Aquifer. The water rushing through vents under the low-water crossing was clear and cold. There was a still pool downstream of the crossing. Maytubby and Bond walked a few steps along the pool bank opposite the ruts.

Hannah pulled a foot of line from her reel, letting the bobber and hook on the end fall to the ground. A small puff of dust rose from the reel. "This ain't gonna cast, Bill."

"I guess we'll just have to pull out slack and lasso out the rig."

Hannah stripped off more line, gingerly. "If this broke-dick line don't snap." She bent, picked up the bobber, sinker, and hook, and slung them into the pool.

Maytubby followed suit. They reeled their lines more or less taut.

"Let's make it look right," Hannah said. She found a Y-shaped branch, stuck the leg in the ground, and laid the rod in its crotch. Maytubby did the same. "You know them hooks are too big for anything in this creek."

They walked back to the road. "What if the game warden comes?" Hannah said. "I don't have a license. You?"

"No. Or any cash. I guess we'll end up in the cell next to the hippies."

"Scrooby would love that," Hannah said. "We'd be out from underfoot." She stopped at the truck to retrieve the nitrile gloves and, from her duty belt, three plastic evidence markers.

They walked on the low-water bridge and stopped before they reached the ruts. A few Styrofoam cups and beer cans littered the creek banks. They continued on the concrete to the other side of the ruts, which were on the downstream side. Then they squatted and studied the road and creek bank. "No casings, no clothes. Nothin'," Hannah said.

"But they might have shot him here and picked up their casings. We'd better steer clear of the ruts." They rose, walked around the ruts, and turned toward the creek bank downstream.

A vehicle engine and crunching gravel from the direction of Ten-Acre Rock halted them. They watched the road. A white Charger nosed down the bank. When it closed on them, Hannah said, "Speak of the devil." She turned sideways to the road and jammed the bright blue gloves and yellow evidence markers in her pants pocket.

Scrooby parked on the bridge and rolled down his window. His face was broad and florid over his black OSBI polo shirt. From ten yards away, Bond and Maytubby could hear his signature exhalation. Hannah called it "the pissed blow." She said to Maytubby, "Make him get out." Maytubby, who was not wearing his cap, raised his hand and pretended to shield his eyes against the sun. He squinted and lowered his head a bit. Hannah stood stock-still and stared at the car.

Agent Dan Scrooby turned his face toward the windshield, puckered, and blew. Then he grunted as he opened the cruiser's door, put one hand on the roof and the other on the top of the door, and hauled himself up and out.

Hannah and Maytubby walked slowly toward him.

The sound of another vehicle approached them. A green pickup made the bridge and stopped. Its driver honked. Scrooby pulled out his badge wallet, flipped it open, and held it aloft. The driver shifted into reverse and gunned the engine, scattering gravel and dirt over the Charger.

"Makin' nice with the locals," Hannah said. "Scrooby all over."

Scrooby blew, shook his head, and stowed the wallet. He ignored the ruts.

Maytubby and Hannah approached him, Maytubby controlling his limp. They stopped. Hannah frowned down at Scrooby. He stuck his thumbs in his belt. "Can I ask what you two are doing so close to our crime scene?"

Maytubby and Bond glanced at each other. So Magaw had not yet told Scrooby about Garn's towing the Focus.

"Fishin'," Hannah said. She turned her eyes to the opposite bank and tilted her head upward.

Scrooby followed her gaze. Then he turned his face back to them and eyed them in turn. "Fishin'," he said with an affected drawl. "What are you using for bait?"

"Cut-up Slim Jims," Maytubby said.

Scrooby blew. "Now I've heard it all." He lowered his head and shook it. He looked off into the woods. "And what do you think you'll catch with that?"

Hannah waited a beat before she said, "Punkinseeds and bullheads. What do you think?"

Scrooby eyed the poles. "Why aren't you minding your rods over there?"

Again Hannah made him wait. "That's why God made bobbers." She stood still and looked down at him. "Me and Bill are enjoyin' the scene-ry."

Scrooby massaged his forehead. "That deputy Magaw sent to guard the crime scene . . ."

"Eph," Hannah said.

"F?"

"Ephraim."

"Joseph's son," Maytubby said. "From the Old Testament."

Scrooby stared at Maytubby. "Oh, yeah, you studied Latin or Greek or something in college." He snorted.

"Greek," Maytubby said. "But the Old Testament was . . ."

Scrooby waved his hand. "Whatever. Anyway, Hannah, where'd you find *that* goober?"

Hannah said nothing.

"He drew his pistol on me! And you know what he said?" Scrooby paused for effect. "'Halt! In the name of the law!'" He opened his eyes wide and let his mouth gape.

Maytubby and Bond managed poker faces.

Scrooby canted his head back and blew like a surfacing whale. "The state brings its considerable resources to darkest Cyclops-land to conduct a professional investigation." He was now talking to himself. "And its agent has to talk down a half-wit deputy." He took in the scene, turned, planted his left hand on the Charger's roof, and lowered himself back into his seat. He slammed the door. The cruiser jounced up Ten-Acre Rock Road and disappeared.

Maytubby and Bond looked at each other and burst out laughing.

"Halt, in the name of the law!" Hannah cackled.

"Eph seen his duty, and he done it," Maytubby said.

"He came near shooting *you*, on the Blue River, when we were after Austin Love."

"'Don't shoot Sergeant Maytubby!'" Maytubby said.

Hannah sobered and resumed searching the ground. "He might have, too," she said softly.

They moved slowly down the stream bank, under the canopy of blackjack and ash, studying the water's edge for anything that had washed down from the Focus. A sounder of feral hogs grunted in the distance.

More Styro cups and french fry pails, a pair of black panties, a moldy OU baseball cap. A second OSBI Charger bumped over the crossing and disappeared. "Looks like Oklahoma City is done with the crime scene," Hannah said.

"*That* one anyway," Maytubby said.

They came to a barbed wire fence, two of its crooked posts suspended in the air over the creek. "Well, shit," Hannah said. "No search warrant." She smiled faintly. They stood at the fence and looked over both downstream banks. Hannah stepped into the creek, duckwalked under the fence.

Maytubby eased his gimp foot into the cold water. When his sneaker jostled the pebbles, silt percolated into the current. Under his heel, he spotted a small bright patch. Likely another Styrofoam chip. He bent and pinched its edges, yanked it from under a larger stone. He pulled his foot from the water and stepped gingerly onto the bank. He still held the object by its edges. Before he read any print on the laminated rectangle, he saw the image of a bison inside a circle—the logo of the US Department of the Interior—and pegged it as a Certificate of Degree of Indian Blood. A CDIB card, in local parlance.

Maytubby shook silt from the card and found the name of its former bearer: Cyrus Mead. Degree of Indian Blood ½. Of the Chickasaw Tribe.

"Bill!" Maytubby looked downstream. Hannah was standing in the stream, pointing to the bank, not two yards beyond the fence. "Black Converse tennis shoe!"

He held the card in the air—again with his fingers only on the edges. Cold water would preserve fingerprints.

"Mead's CDIB card?" she said.

He nodded.

Hannah pulled on a nitrile glove, bent and lifted the shoe from the bank mud, duckwalked it under the fence. Then she laid it on the bank. "I never laid a footprint on the bank past the fence," she said, "so we can fudge this a couple yards." She handed Maytubby a nitrile glove. "Here."

Maytubby laid the CDIB card on the bank. Then he wiggled a hand into the glove. Hannah stuck an evidence marker beside the shoe and the card. They both photographed the shoe and the card and set pins in the mapping program.

Maytubby said, "This card is laminated, but it should go in paper like the wet shoe. We got the liquor bags from Lo—Ms. Mercante. And I have some old crime scene tape behind the pickup seat."

"I guess," Hannah said. She scowled and looked at the ground. "Now I gotta tell my boss. So he can tell that pissant Scrooby."

Maytubby stood quietly for a beat. "Dan comes around. Eventually."

"After he's done blowin'.'"

"And Benny Magaw stood by you when we worked the Verner murder."

Hannah tilted her head and looked at the sky. "Okay. Let's sack these bastards and tape the scene." She paused and looked at Maytubby.

He read her mind. "You think the maggots got his driver's license—or it's still in the car?"

She nodded once. "If they got it, they could find his kinfolk."

"We didn't find a wallet," Maytubby said. "A lot of young people don't carry one. And he wouldn't have a credit card. The CDIB card would have nailed him as a real threat—if Princess and Red could get that. They might have thrown it in the creek after they saw it. Or, what's more likely . . ."

"Cy told them why he was on the property. And then they couldn't care less about a card," Hannah said.

"Which still leaves us with a missing driver's license." Maytubby looked at the creek water sifting through the crossing vents under the road. "You think Princess and Red would scorch the earth?"

"Run Cy's kin to ground? I hope they're too dumb," Hannah said. "But I don't know."

As they were walking back to the pickup, Maytubby said, "You reckon Magaw will send Eph to guard this?"

"Him or Katz. Either one of 'em three eggs short of a dozen. I'd perfer Eph just 'cause he's a burr under Scrooby's saddle." She walked a few steps, then said, "They get paid more'n me."

Maytubby stopped. "No."

"Yessir. They were hired after me. And they're men."

Maytubby was stunned. "You graduated first in our CLEET class, Hannah. You're more qualified to be the sheriff of this county than Magaw."

Bond faced him. "If you could vote in this county, I might get two votes—you and LeeRoy. If LeeRoy voted. I'm rough as a cob. You see me joinin' the Tishomingo First Baptist Church and the Lions Club?"

"No," Maytubby said.

She nodded once. "Let's reel in our lines and weigh our whoppers."

The barbs of the rusted hooks were broken off, the Slim Jim bait taken. Maytubby and Bond settled the rods in the pickup bed, stowed their evidence, and taped the crime scene.

CHAPTER 17

Maytubby stopped at Hannah's house so she could carry her duty belt inside. On her way into the house, she unsnapped her glove pouch and pocketed the last of her nitrile gloves.

Then they drove to Garn's garage. "Lemme talk to him first," Hannah said. Before she reached the open garage door, Garn walked out to greet her. He was wiping his hands on a red shop rag. "Hidey," he said, and stuck the rag in his back pocket. "Got your window glass delivered from a junkyard in Sulphur. What I was tryin' to tell you before. Bitch seatin' it in the regulator, but I got 'er done. Jury-rigged your bumper with zip ties. White ones," he said, beaming, "so you'll hardly notice. Found an old tire your size and mounted it for a spare." He pulled a key from his front pant pocket and handed it to her.

"That was quick. What's the damage?"

"Oh, forty oughta do it."

"Thanks, Garn. I'll bring you a check in about an hour."

He waved it away.

"Listen, Garn . . ." She nodded toward Maytubby's pickup. "Sergeant Maytubby and I have to put crime scene tape around that Focus you towed. I'm sorry, but some state investigators are gonna come calling on you."

Garn frowned, yanked the shop rag out of his back pocket, and began to twist it in his hands.

"Don't worry, Garn. Nothin' about you. They'll just ask about when you towed the Focus. Then they'll examine the vehicle for evidence."

Garn didn't seem reassured. "If you say so, Hannah." He turned and walked back to the garage, still wringing the shop rag.

As Bond and Maytubby strung the tape, she said, "Garn's privacy fence around the tow lot should keep out meddlers. I don't think we need a guard."

"I don't think so," Maytubby said. "Fence has seen better days. But probably not."

Bond tied off the last bit of tape. "Garn got his back up when the city council made him build that fence."

———————

Sheriff Magaw's cruiser and a personal car, a silver Ford SUV, were parked at the Johnston County Courthouse when Maytubby parked his pickup in the lot and turned off the ignition. He said, "You want me along?"

Hannah bent and grabbed the four evidence bags. When she had straightened up, she paused and looked out the front windshield. "Nah," she said. She lifted the door handle with her pinkie. When she was standing outside, she said, "I bet you're goin' to Kingston."

"Make hay while the sun shines," he said.

She nodded, shut the door with her elbow, and walked toward the courthouse. Maytubby started the truck and drove away.

Bond carried the bags into the hallway. She paused at the dispatcher's desk. "He in?" she said.

"Maybe," the dispatcher said.

Bond carried the bags to the sheriff's empty office and set them on his desk. She eyed the bags and pondered her duty. LeeRoy had not told the OSBI officer that she was at his house when Princess and Red came after him.

She listened to hushed voices down the hall, then footsteps. Benny Magaw walked into his office holding a Styrofoam coffee cup. He turned and shut the door. When he walked past Bond, he left a wake of Old Spice. She noticed he was freshly shaved. In the late afternoon.

When he was seated behind his desk, he took a sip of coffee and set the cup down. "Do you want to have a seat, Hannah, or do you intend to tower over me as usual?"

Bond caught a whiff of conciliation and sat in the padded metal chair. Still, she crossed her arms.

Magaw said, "The hermit couple—their names are Stan and Marva Echols—got a lawyer. God knows how. A long-haired scarecrow with a droopy mustache. He got them out on a bail bond and drove them away in a hail-dented green Chevy Cruze. I ran the plate and googled him. Fisk Bortel, Oklahoma City. South Texas College of Law. Passed the Oklahoma bar two years ago."

Bond nodded once.

He surveyed the evidence bags and ran an index finger up and down his forehead. "You—and I assume Sergeant Maytubby—have been busy. Horning in on the state's case."

Bond said nothing.

Magaw said, "I called Agent Scrooby a few minutes ago and told him about the Focus in Garn's lot. He asked me a lot of questions you didn't tell me the answers to. You put me in a fix, Hannah." He tapped the top of one of the paper bags. "And now it looks like the fix is turning into a bind."

Bond unfolded her arms, grasped her thighs, and leaned forward. "The blacksmithing hippies—the Echolses—are living on Chickasaw land. Friend of mine is a female landman who looked up the whatchacallit." Bond rolled her eyes up to find the term. "Homestead patent. They've been there a long time and may intend to claim it. Sergeant Maytubby and I think they do. That'd make 'em squatters. The forty acres was an allotment granted to an ancestor of a teenager named Cy Mead, who we think is the body in the charcoal kiln. We found out from Bill's great-aunt in Cairo that Mead was nosing around in the old Dawes rolls here in this courthouse."

Magaw leaned back in his chair and set his fingertips on the desk.

"The Focus Garn towed from the low-water crossing on Rocky Creek is owned by Cy Mead's family, maybe by him. Bill—Sergeant Maytubby—and I walked the creek downstream from the crossing and found a tennis shoe and Cy Mead's CDIB card. We think the shoe might match a melted one in the charcoal kiln." Bond leaned forward and touched the tops of the plastic bag and the Sooner Foods paper sack on Magaw's desk. "We set evidence markers and taped the scene for OSBI. We also dropped GPS mapping pins. We'll send you those and some others so you can pass 'em along to Scrooby."

Magaw winced, moved his hands to the arms of his chair. "Others," he said grimly.

"The guys in the black GMC pickup who ran LeeRoy Sickles off the road—the truck Jake, uh, Trooper Renaldo chased and lost—they burglarize drugstores. They were storing their loot in a shed behind the Echols house."

"The opioids Scrooby confiscated."

"Yeah," Hannah said. "LeeRoy didn't tell the OSBI folks I was at his house when the GMC showed up past midnight."

"Keeping you out of Dutch. Cagey."

"Anyway," Hannah said, "there were two guys in the truck . . ."

Magaw raised his right hand and made the "Halt" gesture. "Scrooby already briefed me on that encounter. Tall guy in a princess mask, short redhead, entry ram, Sickles blasting away, and so on."

"We know where their house is. On Chadwick Road. Another pin. Don't know their names yet. Stolen plate on the GMC. I parked across the road to watch 'em late last night. Got ready to follow 'em when they were leaving, but they spotted my Buick and thought I was neckers. Smashed my window and stabbed a tire before they drove off. Bill warned Jake Renaldo they might rob another drugstore, and looks like they did. Kingston. Jake got a call, saw the damage and reported it."

Magaw shifted in his chair. Bond saw sweat blooming on the pits of his uniform shirt.

"You're gonna have to write somethin' down in a minute," she said. She waited for Magaw to grab a pencil and a legal pad. "When Bill and I were on the road back from passin' by the Mead house on the other side of Coalgate, we saw the maggots in the GMC. *This* side of Coalgate. They were bein' chased by an early-seventies purple Barracuda." She waited for Magaw to scribble. "The 'Cuda got ahead and cut off the GMC. The guys in the 'Cuda are no-account twins named Larry and Jerry O'Hara."

She waited again for Magaw to jot the names. He laid down his pencil and said, "How did you learn . . ."

Bond waved that away. "In a minute. Bill and I hung back and stopped. Larry and Jerry got out of the 'Cuda and laid down on Princess and Red with assault rifles. I was watchin' 'em through my Steiners. They took the maggots' pistols and pulled some bags, prob'ly the drugs from the robbery, out of the bed of the GMC and put 'em in the 'Cuda. Bill kicked his old Ford around the GMC and tailed the 'Cuda. Larry and Jerry threw one of the pistols out the driver's window. After we followed the 'Cuda to Larry and Jerry's stash shack—that's another pin, by Coalgate Reservoir—we went back and got the maggots' pistol. That's the last pin I'm sendin' you, where we found the pistol." She tapped the tops of the other two sacks. "The unloaded pistol and cartridges are in these. A Kimber forty-five. Bill's liquor store gal in Coalgate ID'd Larry and Jerry, who'd tried to shoplift Mad Dog from her shop. She told us where they lived—another pin. I found melted syringes in a fire pit in front of their trailer. Hold on."

Bond pulled out her phone, swiped and tapped. Magaw reached for his coffee cup but pulled back his hand.

"There," she said, and stowed her phone. "I sent you all the map pins." She heard his phone buzz, and she stood. "Can you tell Chief Fox what I told you?"

Magaw stared at the evidence bags. "Shouldn't Sergeant Maytubby . . ."

"Bill has gone to Kingston in his pickup."

"I see." Magaw pinched his nose and nodded slightly. "I can do that."

Bond said, "I'm takin' personal leave tomorrow. I got at least a month saved up."

Magaw made eye contact without lifting his face. "If that's Indian land and there's an Indian victim, the US Attorney will be relying on OSBI's work. Scrooby is proud, and he hates meddlers."

Bond looked at the blank wall behind his head. She stood silent.

The sheriff pushed himself up from his chair. "I'll send Eph to guard the Rocky Creek crime scene until OSBI gets there." There was a gleam of mirth in his eyes.

Bond said, "Eph . . ."

"I know. 'Halt in the name of the law!'"

Bond smiled and turned toward the door.

"Hannah," Magaw said.

She turned back to him.

"Scrooby didn't mention Indian Country. I don't think it crossed his mind. Who thought of that?"

"LeeRoy Sickles," she said.

CHAPTER 18

Maytubby crossed the rusty Washita south of Tishomingo and threaded cattle pastures of native bluestem and grama grass. Fence-rows of golden hackberries blazed in the afternoon sun. He passed a metal-siding Baptist bookstore and some brick ranch houses. On a deserted stretch, his eye caught what looked like a large whitetail buck grazing in a field. Then he did a double take, hit his brakes, and pulled to the grass shoulder. The animal in the pasture was a bull elk.

Maytubby was thunderstruck. He had never seen elk in the Chickasaw Nation.

He knew of the small wild herd in the eastern part of the Arbuckle Mountains. This bull must be a stray bachelor from that herd, wandering after the earlier rut.

Maytubby also knew that when the Chickasaws were removed from their Mississippi homeland, they were still hunting elk there, and they found elk roaming their newly assigned lands in Indian Territory. That was long ago. Before Anglo hunters ravaged the megafauna. All the bison and most of the elk in Oklahoma now were sired by transplants.

For Maytubby, this rogue bull, with its stately rack of antlers, stirred a little hope—that the elk would venture farther into their old grounds and reclaim them.

His reverie was broken by flashing brake lights on the highway, cars pulling over, their passengers emerging with cell phones to photograph the bull. The elk raised its head, turned, cantered into an oak grove, and disappeared. The gawkers pointed to the field and shouted to one another. Then they got back in their cars and drove away.

Maytubby wished Jill had been there to see the elk with him. He reached for his phone, then put it down.

As pickups towing cattle trailers and horse trailers whooshed past him, he imagined his way back into Jill's ancestors' lives in Mississippi. Some were Chickasaws, like half of him. Jill had a CDIB card like Maytubby's and the murdered Cy Mead's. She was a member of the tribe. Others of her ancestors were African slaves of the Chickasaws. Their descendants, those without Indian blood, had never been recognized by his tribe, though the feds had granted them land after the Civil War. Had those slaves back in Mississippi, Maytubby wondered, butchered the tribe's elk, scraped and stretched the hides for blankets and coats? He didn't know. Neither Maytubby nor his fiancée had researched their genealogy at the nation's cultural center, and they knew why: Maytubby's Chickasaw ancestors might have owned her African ancestors.

He picked up his phone and summoned the Chickasaw dictionary. The word for "elk" was missing. Lost.

The Mead case spilled back into his mind. He shifted into first, checked the traffic, and drove toward Kingston.

The pharmacy was boarded with plywood, draped with crime scene tape. An OSBI cruiser—not Scrooby's—was parked near the side door. An elderly man wearing a red polka-dot welder's cap swept glass shards across the lot with a push broom. A pickup with glass racks was parked on the side of the pharmacy. The glazier plied a retractable tape measure, licked his wooden pencil before he wrote the plate glass dimensions in a spiral notebook he held pinned against the brick facade.

Maytubby drove a few miles east of Kingston to a Chickasaw Travel Stop and its adjoining casino. It catered to Lake Texoma tourists. He entered the convenience store and caught a whiff of cigarette smoke when a patron opened the glass door to the casino. The store was brightly lit and immaculate. The lake's high season was long past, and the place was almost empty. Faint but constant electronic ditties and fanfares, all in the cheerful key of C, drifted from the busy casino.

He waved to the counter clerks and checked his limp as he approached the security guard standing by the glass casino door—a tall, thin young man with black hair and a wispy mustache. The young man smiled and nodded. Maytubby smiled and said, "I'm Sergeant Maytubby. Off duty." He took out his badge wallet, held it up, and put it away.

The guard stood up straight and said, "Lighthorse, yessir!" He glanced inside the casino and cast an uneasy look at Maytubby.

Maytubby waved a calming hand. "There's no problem . . ." He glanced at the name tag. ". . . Mr. Enubby. Do you know who was working this door graveyard last night?"

"I was," Enubby said. "Just came back on shift." He looked over Maytubby's head and mouthed *It's okay* to the store clerks.

Maytubby said, "You can see the store side and the casino side. That's good. You know the pharmacy in Kingston was broken into late last night."

"Yessir," Enubby said. He looked around Maytubby. "Excuse me, sir." A girl stepped toward the casino door. Enubby blocked her. "I need to see your ID, ma'am."

"Oh, really? C'mon, man." She grinned at him and tried to shoulder him aside.

Enubby grabbed her arm and pulled her back into the store.

She pulled her arm free. "Fuck you!" she shouted, and stormed away.

Enubby shook his head and turned back to Maytubby. "Sorry, Sergeant."

"Doing your job right." He watched Enubby mash his lips and nod with pride. "Did you see a pair of guys—they were driving a black GMC pickup—tall, dark fellow and a shorter redheaded one with a red goatee beard?"

Enubby searched the floor a few seconds. Then he shook his head. "No. I'm sorry," he said.

"*Yakoke*," Maytubby said. "You know what that means?"

Enubby smiled. "Yeah."

Maytubby turned to walk away, stopped, and faced Enubby again. "You ever see an old hippie couple on a motorcycle with fat saddlebags?"

Enubby brightened. "Yeah, they been in the store but not the casino."

"When's the last time you saw them?"

Enubby pulled at a corner of his mustache. "One, two . . . Four nights ago. They bought a few things at the register. They were stinky. I could smell 'em over the smoke."

"Did you notice if they asked the store clerks any questions?"

"Let's find out," Enubby said. He took a step away from the door. Maytubby turned and saw there were no customers at the counter. "Hey, guys," Enubby said. He pointed at Maytubby. "This is a Lighthorseman. Undercover." Maytubby smiled at the word. "You remember those smelly old hippies on the motorcycle four nights ago?"

The clerks, a young man and a young woman, said, "Yeah," in unison. The young woman said, "Wearing Confederate flag do-rags. Filthy ones."

"They ask anything about the pharmacy that was burglarized last night?" Enubby said.

The young woman, who had a small tattoo on her arm, said, "The lady said she needed to fill a prescription, and asked when it closed. I told her five o'clock. It was already closed. The hours are painted on the door, or she could have looked it up on her phone."

"If a hippie like that had one. What did they buy?" Enubby said.

The clerks looked at each another, and the young man spoke. "Two gallon cans of Coleman fuel and lantern mantles. I didn't see how those cans could fit in the saddlebags. Guess they did."

Enubby said, "No room for camping gear on that bike, so they weren't going to the lake. How'd they pay?" Maytubby was going to ask just that.

"Two twenties," the young woman said. "From a biker wallet on a chain."

Enubby said, "Could you see if he had a lot of cash?"

"Oh, yeah," the young man said. "Big wad." His partner nodded.

Enubby turned from them. "You have some questions, Sergeant?"

"No. You asked the right ones," Maytubby said. They took a few steps to the casino door. "Are you going to college?"

Enubby took his post, looked briefly into the casino. "Yessir. Majoring in criminal justice at Southeastern. Online. I'm a junior."

"Good. You cut to the chase," Maytubby said. "When you graduate, if you're interested in the Lighthorse, call me at the headquarters in Ada. I'll put in a word for you."

Enubby's eyes widened. "Yessir, Lighthorse Sergeant. I mean, Sergeant Maytubby. I will."

Maytubby thanked the clerks as he left the store. In his pickup, he tossed back some dried cranberries and parsed the clerks' news. If the ironsmiths were scouting the pharmacy for Princess and Red— and if Princess and Red did rob the place last night—the job was planned well before OSBI raided the shack. Maytubby's heads-up for Trooper Renaldo was dumb luck. The Sulphur Walmart sold Coleman fuel and mantles a lot cheaper than this CTS, and it was twenty miles closer to the charcoal forge house. On the other hand, LeeRoy Sickles had claimed the "weirdo couple," as he called them, bought their supplies from small towns so they could remain anonymous on their home turf. The travel stop would fit that bill.

CHAPTER 19

Maytubby started his pickup and drove back into Kingston. The crime scene tape was gone from the pharmacy, as was the OSBI cruiser. A Kingston Police prowler idled in the lot. Maytubby cruised the town streets. When he came to the high school, the Redskins football team was practicing on the field, linemen shouldering a blocking sled while a coach shouted at them. On an adjacent field, the marching band drilled under the eye of their director, who barked into a bullhorn.

Maytubby noticed, near the school's front door, two people standing atop extension ladders, busy with a changeable letter marquee on a steel pole. When he neared their pickup, he saw "Rummel Scoreboards Sales and Service" on the driver's door. They would be on the watchtowers. He memorized the business name and phone number, parked, and watched as they removed a shattered polycarbonate sheet and carried it down between them. A man and a woman in late middle age, both with short white hair and both wearing new crimson OU ball caps.

Maytubby rolled down his window so he could listen. They carried the ruined sheet to their pickup and returned with a new pane, mounted their ladders, and walked it up between them. Once the clear sheet was in place, they stepped up one rung and slid the REDSKINS header a foot or so to their left, exposing a darkened fluorescent tube. The woman pulled on gloves, gave the smutched tube a half twist. She descended the ladder with the burned-out light, swapped it for a new one in the pickup bed, and went up again. Neither said a word; they were dancing to an old tune.

While the woman replaced the bulb, Maytubby called Jake Renaldo.

"Hey, Jake. I'm in Kingston."

"Holding OSBI's feet to the fire, eh?"

"I didn't talk to 'em, but I saw the car at the drugstore. Just off the top of your head, where were there small-town pharmacy burglaries or robberies in Troop F recently?" Troop F roughly matched the Chickasaw Nation boundaries.

"Lessee. A couple in Ada, but you know about those."

"Little towns," Maytubby said.

"Oh. Allen, Madill. Uh, a little east, in Troop E—Coalgate, Antlers." Renaldo paused. "Huh. That's a lot."

"Hold-ups or burglaries?"

"All burglaries," Renaldo said.

"Thanks, Jake. You've given me a seam to mine, like your Italian ancestor."

"Hope it's better than soft coal in the Pinch-Along. Lemme know." Jake ended the call.

Maytubby combed his hair with his fingers, got out of the pickup, and limped toward the tall couple. The woman was taking off her gloves.

He smiled. "Hi. I'm Bill Maytubby."

The couple smiled, unperturbed. The woman said, "I'm Jenny, and this is my husband, Hal." They all shook hands. "How can we help you?" Jenny said. She glanced at his game leg.

"I'm a tribal police officer, technically off duty . . ." He started to reach for his badge.

"Lighthorse. We're in Kingston, so, Chickasaw?" Hal said.

Maytubby let the badge alone. "Yes," he said.

Jenny said, "We know Chief Fox. He's a big Ada Cougars booster. We've worked on their scoreboard for a coon's age."

"Seems like that Plexiglas would be hard to break."

"Real hard," Hal said. "I didn't believe it." He took a step back, reached into the pickup bed, and pulled up an unopened amber long-neck. "Laying in the bottom of the marquee."

"Twisted physics." Maytubby said. "Listen, I'm investigating some pharmacy break-ins in the area. There was one here in Kingston last night."

Jenny and Hal looked surprised.

"In your business," Maytubby said, pointing at the marquee, "you're up high. You see folks coming and going."

The couple looked at each other and tittered. Jenny said, "We mostly have our nose in wiring and bulbs. Whatcha got?"

Maytubby said, "In the last couple months, have you worked on football or baseball scoreboards in Allen, Coalgate, Antlers, or Madill?" A coach's whistle shrilled from the practice field. "There have been pharmacy burglaries in all those towns."

That got their attention. "Madill and Allen, yeah," Hal said. "Football scoreboards."

Maytubby said, "The stadium in Madill, as I remember, is about six blocks south of the downtown pharmacies."

"Yeah," Jenny said, "but there's a lot of big oak trees in between that stadium and downtown."

"I'll try anyway," Maytubby said. He skipped the GMC—too common. "A purple seventies Barracuda."

They looked at each other and shook their heads.

"Old hippie couple on a motorcycle with big saddlebags."

Again they shook their heads. But Jenny wrinkled her nose and glanced at her feet. Hal looked at his watch.

Maytubby said, "The Allen football stadium is closer to downtown."

The Redskin band struck up "Hit Me with Your Best Shot."

Hal shook his head. "Sorry, Officer, but we need to get to a job in Stonewall before dark." He moved toward the ladders.

"Wait . . ." Jenny pulled off her cap and jiggled it toward Sam. "Go ahead and get the ladders, hon. I'm remembering something." Hal nodded and took hold of a ladder.

Jenny shook out her short hair and dropped the cap to her side. "About two weeks ago. That was a control module job. 'Down' numbers dark. What you said about the saddlebags jogged my memory." She turned to watch her husband retract the extension. "That black motorcycle drove to the stadium from downtown." She faced Maytubby and tilted her head. "If you can call anything in Allen 'downtown.' Hal and I had to replace a TRIAC card in the module. They parked below us—out about, oh, twenty yards. Yeah, yeah!" She grew excited. "They got off the cycle and started rolling—I thought they were joints, but when they lit up I could smell it was cigarettes. They weren't wearing helmets. They had neckerchiefs tied over their heads, tails hanging down."

"Do-rags," Maytubby said.

Jenny shrugged. "Whatever they're called. Rebel flag pattern. Dirty. The guy had one of those black chain purse things on his belt. Hal was replacing the panel cover. When I looked down again, they had a big paper tablet like artists use laid out on the cycle seat. The woman had a pencil or pen, writing on the paper. The man pointed to the tablet. They smoked and seemed to argue about something."

"Could you . . . ?"

She shook her head. "They didn't yell. Anyway, they threw their butts on the ground, the woman folded up the paper and put it in a saddlebag, and they drove off. West, away from town. Real slow. No *vroom-vroom* like they do."

Maytubby said, "Thank you, ma'am. Your information has been very helpful." He pulled out his wallet and handed her his card. "If you remember anything else, please call me."

Jenny took the card and slid it into her front jeans pocket. Hal carried a ladder behind her, lifted it, and settled it into a truck-bed rack. She put on her OU cap. "You got it," she said. She waved, turned, and fell in step with Hal as they went to fetch the second ladder.

Maytubby favored his hurt foot as he climbed into his pickup. He watched the Rummels stow the second ladder. They laced their arms over each other's shoulders and looked up to appraise their work. Then they kissed and tousled each other's hair, their autumn shadows long on the school pavement.

The Pride of Texomaland hit the opening bars of "Oklahoma!"

Maytubby followed the Rummels north out of Kingston. Their pickup soon vanished up the road to Stonewall.

The sunset glare, on his left, forced him to pull over so he could call Hannah.

"Bill," she said. "I'm home right now. I told Magaw everything we know. He's not happy, but I think he's on our side."

"This early in the game?"

"Yup."

"Think LeeRoy romanced him?"

"Heh heh. Maybe. The weird couple are Stan and Marva Echols. You learn anything?"

"Yes. The weird couple on the motorcycle—the Echolses. They were in Kingston, asking about the pharmacy four days before the burglary. Before that, they were in Allen before a drugstore burglary there—one Jake told me about. Maybe sketching tactics."

"Growin' a callus on your soft spot for the squatters?"

"I am."

"Good. Garn fixed the Buick. I'm goin' out to snoop on the maggots soon as it gets dark. You on the road to your girlfriend's house?"

"If she'll have me. Talk to you later." Hannah ended the call.

The sun had set. Maytubby put his cell on speaker and told it to call Jill. He laid the phone on the bench seat, checked traffic, and nosed onto the highway.

"I thought I blocked this number," Jill Milton said.

"Road to hell paved with unblocked numbers."

"Don't you dare bring up that fire-eater from Texarkana."

"You mean Dude, your Brooklyn hipster friend? Farthest thing from my mind."

"Can you pick up cilantro and deli mozzarella from Dicus Apple Market?"

"Yes. You didn't block Dude's number?"

"And a bottle of Chardonnay," Jill said.

"To pair with the truffled capon," Maytubby said.

"If you can find truffled capon in Ada, sure."

In the dun twilight, Maytubby passed a barred owl perched on a crooked fencepost. "Shows what you know. The Walmart deli is a truffled-capon factory."

"I need to get out more."

CHAPTER 20

Bond struck a wooden match and lit the burner under a pan of cold coffee. While the coffee heated, she wrote a check for forty dollars to Garner's Garage. She tore the check out, folded it, and slipped it into her shirt pocket. When the coffee was hot, she poured it into a thermos. On her cell, she called Gonzalez Restaurant and ordered a grande beef burrito to go. She carried the thermos and her duty belt to the Skylark. The Steiners were already on the bench seat.

Bond parked beside several cars in front of Garn's garage. A clam-shell lamp dangled from a broken mast, illuminating a patch of stucco about a foot below the REPAIRS sign. Inside the open garage door, the corona of a trouble light glowed around the edges of a raised car hood.

She got out of the Skylark and slammed the door to give him some notice. She didn't want to appear at his side while he was working. Garn was a jumpy guy.

A vehicle drove slowly behind her on the street. She turned and caught a glimpse of it as it accelerated into the darkness. A new, big SUV. Dark paint. Maybe a Lincoln Navigator. Nobody in Tish owned one.

"With you in a minute," he called as she walked toward the car in the bay. The shop smelled of gasoline and exhaust. Bugs spun around the trouble light, which hung from the hood latch.

"Hey, Garn," she said softly when she stood by him.

Garn didn't look up. "Hey, Hannah." He was securing a belt tensioner. "Gol-dern serpent belts on these new engines. It's like a rodeo barrel race . . ." He strained and grunted. "Only with a lot more barrels." He straightened up and set his ratchet gently on the radiator guard. "Done," he said. He wiped sweat from his face with his sleeve, slid the ratchet into his pocket, clicked off the trouble light, hung it on a hose rack, and closed the hood. He pulled a shop rag from his pocket and wiped his hands. Then he took a few steps to a stained sink and washed his hands with a green bar of Lava soap. He dried them on the legs of his coveralls.

Hannah took the check from her shirt pocket, unfolded it, and handed it to him. He took the check and nodded toward an old library table surrounded by metal filing cabinets. He sat on a stool and flicked on the table light.

"I don't need a receipt, Garn," Hannah said.

Garn slid a tablet of auto repair carbon forms across the table and unfolded a pair of drugstore reading glasses. "This is for the taxman, Hannah." He held the check in his left hand and tapped numbers into a plastic calculator. With each result, he nodded but wrote nothing until he sat back down and clicked a ballpoint pen. Hannah realized he was memorizing the figures, like her friend Maytubby. Garn swiftly entered parts, labor, and tax. The TOTAL box was an even forty bucks. She saw that the LABOR line was $3.00.

Garn endorsed the check and dropped it in the desk's top drawer. He tore off the order form, handed her the carbon, and filed the original.

"You done for the night, Garn?"

He lowered his face and rolled his eyes up to her. "You saw them cars out front?"

"Yeah."

"Two brake jobs before I can call it a night. Everbody's in a big hurry."

"Any agents come to look at the Focus?"

Garn's eyes flicked toward the back of the shop. "Not yet. I don't like the thought."

"Garn, that DUI in high school was thirty years ago."

"And I—"

"I know you haven't. The agents won't know a thing about that."

Garn removed his glasses and laid them on the library table. "Okay, Hannah. I trust you."

"Thanks for patchin' up the Buick." She caught his eye. "Three dollars," she said.

"Not so long ago, that was a week's grocery money," he said flatly. "See ya." He turned to lift a tagged key ring from its peg on the schedule board.

Bond walked out of the garage, got in the Skylark, and drove to Gonzalez Restaurant. Ruperto met her at the door with a paper sack. Hannah gave him a ten and told him to keep the change. Ruperto smiled and nodded. "*Gracias. Cuídate.*"

Bond unwrapped the burrito and polished it off before she hit the city limits on her way to Chadwick Road. Maytubby had put the Echolses in cahoots with Princess and Red. The Texas lawyer had sprung the old toolmakers, the kiln house was hot, and nobody but her and Maytubby and Magaw knew about the Chadwick Road house, so the odds there'd be a convention going on were good. Save her sneaking up on the kiln house through the woods. She drove past wind towers. The moonlit slabs of their nacelles reminded her of the marble tombstones in a pioneer cemetery where she had slept when her foster father got gibbering drunk.

Bond turned onto Samson Road and passed silica conveyors lit bright as day. The SUV driving by Garn's garage preyed on her mind. She pulled to the side of the gravel road and called the Johnston County sheriff's dispatcher. She learned that Katz was on duty. Though he was the steadier of the two loose cannons, it was cold comfort. "Could you ask him to drive by Garn's garage ever so often? Garn's holding a vehicle for evidence back in his yard."

The lights of Sulphur glowed along the western horizon. The road made right angles along section lines to Chadwick Road. When she neared the house, she slowed for a first pass.

"Damn," she said. "Morons left the porch light on again." Every last wild horse in the roundup—the black GMC, the old red Chevy, the black Harley with its fat saddlebags, the lawyer's Cruze. Headlights from a tall vehicle coming the opposite way lit the Buick's cab. When it passed her, she took care not to hit her brakes. Her own headlights showed her a black Navigator. In her rearview, she saw its brake lights flash just as it turned into the maggots' drive. The plate lamp was dark, but the brake lights showed an Oklahoma tag. *That's money,* Bond thought. If the Texas lawyer had an Oklahoma City address, the Navigator likely did, too. She would bet the SUV plate wasn't stolen. Rich people wouldn't dirty their hands.

Bond drove slowly. She passed the kindly rancher's gate. If the Navigator was parked beyond the porch light, she could read its tag with her Steiners. The rancher watched his gate, and might interfere if she parked there and walked the road to the maggots' drive. "Well, shit," Bond said.

She made a three-point turn and drove back toward the house. She hadn't seen a guard—on the porch or at the road—and the gang would be busy in the house. When she reached the drive, she turned off her headlights, stopped, and trained her binoculars on the SUV. Its plate caught the porch light and yielded its number. She drove away, navigated by moonlight until she saw a single tree bending over the road. Scant cover, but it still had leaves and would cast a moon shadow over her white car. She made another three-point turn and parked.

She cranked down her window, looked up and saw the pods and long thorns of a honey locust silhouetted against the moon. "Huh," she said. The same trees shaded the cemetery where she slept, and in the late autumn she had cracked open the shed pods and licked out the sweet pulp to stave off hunger. "Old home week," she said.

Bond could not see the house, only the end of the driveway. She got out her cell and ran the Navigator tag. As she had reckoned, it matched the vehicle. Mitchell Searcy, Deer Creek, Oklahoma. "Damn," she whispered. The guy Patty said owns the land around the squatters. Deer Creek—rich acreage people, as she recalled. Oklahoma City commuters. She sent a text with the ID to Magaw and put her phone away. She would tell Maytubby later. She drank coffee from her thermos. When the moon shadow crept east, she started her car and backed it into shade.

Just after eleven, an engine roared to life. It revved three times. The old Chevy pickup. Bond started the Buick, turned on her headlights, and accelerated toward the driveway. When she passed it, two sets of headlights approached the road. She pulled into the kindly rancher's drive, stopped, got out of the car, and walked toward the gate as if she owned the place. The Navigator blew past, headed for the City. Through its dust, she saw the Chevy's single taillight fade toward the east.

Bond folded herself into the Skylark and pursued the Chevy, her headlights off, steering by moonlight. The Chevy neared sixty, slewed wildly at every dogleg. Bond shook her head. At the last hard left, the pickup spun out into the bar ditch. Bond drove past it, waited a beat, and turned on her headlights. She parked in the quarry lot and waited for the pickup. When it passed her and turned south on the Tish highway, she gave it a quarter mile before she followed.

The Chevy pounded through Mill Creek, past the Ten-Acre Rock turnoff. In Ravia, it turned away from the Washita toward Tishomingo. Eight minutes. Bond pulled out her cell and called the dispatcher. "Tell Katz to go to the back fence of Garn's garage right now. Tell him . . ."

"Sheriff Magaw's already at Garn's garage," the dispatcher said.

Bond throttled her surprise. Magaw didn't work at night. "Radio the sheriff and tell him to block the alley behind Garn's fence. Tell him to look for a seventies red Chevy pickup. I'm tailing it past Ravia." She ended the call, pulled her duty belt from the passenger floorboard, and slid the holster next to her on the bench seat. She was glad she had told Benny Magaw about the Focus in Garn's lot. Magaw would catch on when the dispatcher radioed him. He was also a cool hand. Bond decided to let Magaw warn Garn. She sped over Sand Creek and Pennington Creek, gaining on the single taillight.

The Chevy ran two red lights in downtown Tish. Bond checked for cross traffic before she ran them, too. Streetlights silhouetted a tall, heavy man. Princess and not Red. The pickup fishtailed on a left turn. Bond broke the tail for a shortcut to Garn's. When she got to the alley, there was no sign of Magaw's cruiser or the pickup. She did not stop but circled the block.

Bond spotted the sheriff parked in an offset of the alley behind Garn's, across the street. He had a good view of the lot's privacy fence, faintly lit by a hanging barn light. She downshifted the Buick to a crawl and turned off her headlights. Her window was still down. She listened for creaking door hinges. Country music drifted over the neighborhood's cracker-box houses. Did Princess spot her tail and blow out of town on the Ada highway? If he was skulking, she thought, what was his big rush to get here? She idled in the Assembly of God lot and called the sheriff's cell.

"Deputy Bond. What's keeping you and your red Chevy?"

"I been here," Bond said. She scanned the narrow asphalt streets. "Just parked at the Assembly o' God. I left the Chevy going north on Kemp so I could beat him to Garn's."

"Mission accomplished," Magaw said.

"Huh. Yeah."

"Garn's under a Jeep, doing a brake job. I gave him a heads-up."

"Good," Bond said. She held her phone in her lap, waiting for Magaw to respond. Then, off to her left, across Kemp, she heard a throaty engine boom to life. It revved three times. "He's comin' in, Sheriff. On Sixth or Seventh. Out." She ended the call, shifted into first, and tasked the old Buick with a sprint to the garage.

The pickup burst across her path. She gave chase, then hit her brakes for a cat, which leaped straight into the air and hit the ground running. She heard the bang and snap of metal on wood, rounded the corner to find Magaw's cruiser athwart the alley and, in her headlights, the bed of the Chevy pickup rocking to a halt, tented with shorn pickets.

Princess had skirted the alley and breached the lot gate on the street side. He must have spotted the cruiser at the last second. The floodlights on Garn's garage flicked on. As Magaw walked quickly toward the pickup, his service pistol pointed at the ground, Bond snugged the Skylark against the Chevy's tailgate and ducked out of her car with the Model 10. There was smoke in the Chevy's cab. She beat Magaw to the fence, lowered her shoulder, and broke through the rotten pickets wedged against the bed.

Bond stepped free of the fence, Magaw just behind her, and raised her pistol with both hands. She saw the back of a large man. His feet were spread, his arm cocked. In his right hand, a green bottle crowned with flame. The same instant she shouted "Put that down and step back!" she saw the bottle quiver. As he launched the cocktail, its rag fuse broke free. Liquid fire arced in every direction. His right sleeve and pant leg sprouted flames. The bottle fell short of the Focus and splintered on a discarded tire rim. The man bellowed and danced, flailing his arms. Magaw holstered his pistol; Hannah laid hers on the ground. They rushed the man, knocked him down, and rolled him like a barrel. Garn burst from the garage with a powder extinguisher. He fogged patches of flame on the tumbling body, then pivoted and snuffed the tentacles creeping from the tire rim. Not an inch of the crime scene tape on the Focus had melted.

Magaw, on his knees, saw that Bond held the man down by his unsinged biceps. The sheriff touched his shoulder mike and called for an ambulance.

Unleashing a primal yodel, the man writhed free of Bond, flattened his palms on the ground, and sprang up. Garn blasted his face with the extinguisher. Bond threw her shoulder into the arsonist's knees and tackled him. Magaw whipped plasticuffs from his duty belt and pinioned the man's legs. Blisters were rising on the man's hands and forearms. He rolled onto his back and flapped them in the air. A siren pitched up in the distance. Bond stood, and he looked at her face. His red eyes widened, then blinked against the monoammonium phosphate. "The fuckin' sow!" he said, then laughed bitterly as tears leaked toward his ears.

"Howdy, Princess," she said.

"Garn," she said, "fetch some water so I can douse his face." The man coughed and shook his head. Garn solemnly ferried a plastic bucket from the garage and handed it to Bond. "Princess," she said, "keep your eyes open if you can. I'm 'bout to throw this bucket of water in your face. It'll wash off the poison from the far extinguisher." He didn't protest. Bond poured the water gently. "Blink your eyes," she said. He obeyed.

While Bond ministered to Princess, Magaw jiggered out the man's wallet, cell phone, keys, and lighter. "You're under arrest," Magaw said. "For breaking and entering, attempted arson, and resisting arrest." He recited Miranda as he opened the wallet. "Mr. . . . I don't see a license. What's your name?"

The ambulance crunched into the alley. Bond handed the bucket to Garn, walked to the fence by the pickup, and kicked out a half dozen more pickets. "In here," she said. As the EMTs carried the stretcher into the lot, Bond walked beside them, explained the man's injuries, and told them he was under arrest, his legs cuffed.

As the EMTs went to work, Magaw leaned over the prisoner. "Tell me your name," he said. The man shook his head. Magaw said, "When you get to the hospital, you can call your lawyer, Fisk Bortel, from the land line in your room." The man started at the name. He was being jostled by the EMTs. Magaw nodded. "I'm sure he'll tell your friends on Chadwick Road before he gets in his Cruze and hits the road for Tish to bail out your sorry ass. Or not."

Magaw followed the EMTs as they carried his stretcher through the fence. "Fuck!" the man said.

"Yeah," the sheriff said.

Hannah picked up her revolver and stuck it in the waist of her pants, behind her back. She took a few steps to the Chevy and ran her Maglite over the interior. No wallet or driver's license. But she did see what looked like a bullet hole in the passenger headrest. She turned and watched Garn appraising the Chevy. "What d'ya think of that?" she said. "Crook drives right into an impound lot."

"I think I'm out a tow fee, six yards of fence"—he held up the extinguisher—"and forty bucks' worth of juice."

Hannah walked slowly to Garn and laid her hand on his shoulder. "Garn, when Benny Magaw tells the county commissioners you risked your life to take down a felon, I bet they fix you up."

Garn waved the extinguisher nozzle absently.

Through the fence gap, they watched the blue strobes of a cruiser approach. "Has to be Katz," Hannah said. "Overheads for nothin'." Tires squealed. "Sheriff probably sent him here to guard the lot."

Garn shook his head. "Deputy Katz. Just what I need. Sorry, Hannah, but I got to finish a brake job."

"Yeah. Okay," Hannah said. Garn shouldered the extinguisher and trudged back to the shop.

Katz bounded through the hole in the fence and ran to Hannah's side. He yanked off his uniform Western hat, held it at his side and surveyed the damage. "*Phoo-ooo!*" he said, and stomped his foot. "Did you ram that truck through the gate, Hannah? Lookit all that burnt grass! Lucky he didn't burn up that little Focus and Garn's whole garage!" Katz squatted down and reached for the intact neck of the green bottle.

"No, Deputy! This is a crime scene," Bond said. "That's why you're here."

Katz snapped his fingers and then rose. "Why didn't you and Benny shoot that mother?"

"Because he was on fire."

CHAPTER 21

Maytubby parked in the Apple Dicus Grocery lot in Ada. In the twilight, the lot's sodium lamps flickered on. Bullbats swooped between the standards. He still wore his jeans and tatty long-sleeved shirt. The lot was practically empty. A new black Lincoln Navigator caught his eye. Freshly washed and waxed, it was what Hannah would call "stick-out." It was parked away from the other vehicles so it wouldn't get dinged. Maytubby memorized the plate and Oklahoma City dealer decal out of habit. There was a SKI ASPEN sticker on the rear window, as if the vehicle needed more brag.

Maytubby limped into the store. He had lost his distractions, so his toe was giving him grief. He grabbed the last bunch of cilantro in produce, took a few steps to the deli's refrigerated vitrine. There was no clerk at the deli. A tall, fit man stood in front of the vitrine. He was about fifty, had an expensive haircut. Fashionable tortoise-shell glasses. He wore a powder-blue Ralph Lauren polo jacket and chinos, which broke perfectly over cherry-red Doc Martens loafers. His right hand, when he reached for the call bell, was soft and manicured. Clearly the Navigator man, not from around here.

Maytubby took a step back and watched him. The man squatted and surveyed the shelves. He shook his head and sighed. "Garbage," he muttered. He rose, laid his palms on the top of the vitrine, leaned toward it, and hung his head. He lowered his left arm, checked his watch, and sighed. "Fucking hicks," he stage-whispered.

"*Alors,*" Maytubby said softly. The man shoved off the vitrine, spun around, and stared at him.

"*Désolé, nous sommes des ploucs.*" I am sorry we are hicks.

The man looked Maytubby up and down and frowned. "Are you speaking French?"

Maytubby waved the bunch of cilantro. "Yeah. I said I was sorry we're hicks." He watched a clerk he knew stepping quickly toward the back of the vitrine, wiping her hands on an apron. He waved at her and said, "Hey, Vick."

Vicky smiled. "Hey, Bill." She washed her hands in a small sink behind the counter.

The man continued to stare at Maytubby. "Where did you learn to speak French?"

"Ada High," Maytubby half-lied.

Vicky watched them quizzically. Maytubby knew she had been in Jill's French classes.

Maytubby opened his palm upward toward the man and gave her a look. "I was telling this gentleman we all speak French in Ada. Isn't that right, Vick?"

The man turned his face toward her.

"*Mais oui,*" she said gravely, knitting her brow and nodding slowly. She narrowed her eyes a little at Maytubby, warning him she couldn't keep it up. Then she smiled at the man and said, "What can I get you?" as she pulled on food-handler gloves.

After a beat, the man came around. "Oh, uh . . ." He pointed at the glass. "Both those meat party trays. That's all."

Vicky nodded and set the trays on top of the case. "*Merci!*" she said.

When the man turned with his trays, he gave a start, nearly colliding with Maytubby, who hadn't moved.

Maytubby grinned and held his cilantro aloft. "*D'accord!*" he said.

The man stared at him and gave him a wide berth on his way to checkout.

Vicky leaned over the vitrine counter. "What was *that* all about?"

Maytubby checked to be sure the man was out of earshot. "Guy was dissing your deli. Saying we're all hicks. I just turned the tables."

Vicky wrinkled her nose and giggled. She cleared her throat. "Good for you. Damn slicker. Now. What can I get you?"

"A quarter pound of mozzarella, unsliced."

She paused. "What's the magic word?"

"*S'il vous plaît*," he said in the old style.

She nodded. "That's better." As she handed him the cheese, she said, "Poor Madame Corbin. She had a hard life. She was a good teacher. And those bad boys at school made fun of her."

Maytubby took his cheese and blushed. He stifled an urge to come clean. "She did have a hard life." He raised the cheese over his head in salute and said, "See you."

It was full dark when he reentered the parking lot. He realized he wasn't limping. When he saw that the Navigator was gone, his foot began to throb again.

Up Mississippi Street, he pulled into the liquor store where he had bought the half-pint of whiskey. The Navigator was idling there. Maytubby noticed that its plate lamps were out. He turned off his headlights and killed the engine. The store lights showed a silhouette of the rich man talking on his cell. Maytubby waited until the Navigator's driver door opened and the man went inside. He waited a few seconds and followed him in.

A wall of glassed coolers in a liquor store still surprised Maytubby. It had been only a few months since Oklahoma legalized them. And only a few decades since the whole state was dry. A governor who jailed bootleggers got that changed.

The man walked to the domestic beer section of the coolers; Maytubby walked to the few racks devoted to wine. He knew the unoaked Chardonnay he wanted, but waited until the man dragged out a case of Keystone and turned toward the counter. That city snob toting out a weekender of *Keystone*? Maytubby took out his bottle, closed the glass door softly, and walked around the bourbon and vodka aisles so the man wouldn't see him. When the man hefted the beer onto the counter, he said to the owner, "Excuse me, but do you speak French?"

Maytubby peeked around vodka bottles to watch.

The owner dropped his hands from the beer case onto the counter. "Do I *what*?"

"Nothing," the man said. He handed the man a bill and then waved his own question away. The owner passed change over the counter but kept his eye on the man. Maytubby quietly stepped out of the aisle and cradled his wine, label out. When the man lifted his beer off the counter and turned around, Maytubby grinned at him. He stopped in his tracks.

Maytubby looked at the beer. The man followed his gaze and seemed to see his own purchase for the first time. He grew flustered and looked away. Maytubby saw something beyond chagrin in his eyes—a trace of fear.

"This isn't for me," the man said to the air. As he passed Maytubby he said, "I would never drink this swill."

Coming out of the liquor store, Maytubby saw the Navigator turn south on Mississippi. Oklahoma City was north. In his pickup cab, he ran the plate on his phone. Mitchell Searcy. He googled Searcy and found he was the owner of Buck Aviation at Wiley Post Airport. Searcy lived in Deer Creek. The affluent exurb fit the man and his Lincoln. But not the swill.

CHAPTER 22

Maytubby parked at his house and carried the fishing rods to his toolshed. The bulb dangling above his front door cast spider-leg shadows. Inside, it was chilly. He turned on the hot-water tap of his old claw-foot tub, walked into his bedroom, and stripped. He picked his well-thumbed Emily Dickinson off the floor and set it atop his bedside books.

He high-stepped into the tub, bent and turned on the cold tap, picked up a plastic Mardi Gras go-cup Chief Fox had brought him from New Orleans long ago, and moved it back and forth between the hot and cold taps before dumping it over his head. He repeated the process three times and shut off the taps. The warm water eased the pain in his ribs and foot. He was about to reach for the bar soap when he thought of Cy Mead's family. His mother and grandmother, maybe sisters and brothers. As he stood in the chill, dripping water into the tub, he imagined Princess and Red, drunk and rash—or even the axe-forging Echolses, with their rattletrap motorcycle—finding Cy's address on his license and setting out to snuff the last claim to the homestead patent. That seemed extreme and unlikely. But Princess and Red had tracked down LeeRoy Sickles—twice—and he was nothing more than a nuisance.

Maytubby opened the taps and doused himself with the cup once more, lathered his hair and body with the bar soap, and rinsed with two more cups. He closed the taps, toweled off in the tub, sat on its lip, and dressed his toe. Falling pecans popped on his roof and rolled down. In his bedroom, he slid on the jeans he had worn, and tucked in a fresh twill button-down shirt. He slid on clean socks and his trail runners. He lifted his duty belt off the back of a chair and retrieved his goober teeth.

As he reached for the pull cord to switch off the dangling kitchen bulb, he inhaled the scent of sage and fried venison.

He switched off the light and went out the door.

Maytubby drove up to the bluff that shouldered the King's Road oil mansions. Tonight, their facades were veiled by security flood-lights. He drove through the rock driveway pillars of the big house in front of Jill's garage apartment, parked at the base of her stairs, and, favoring his toe, carried up mozzarella, cilantro, wine, and the waxed paper–wrapped slice of pecan pie his great-aunt had given him. On the landing, he heard, instead of Jill's banjo, the voice of Antonia Gonzales on KOUA's *National Native News*.

He backed through the door with his load. Jill walked out of her short hallway carrying the paperback of *Olive Kitteridge*, her index finger in its midsection. She was wearing jeans and a plum pullover sweater, her hair in a chignon. She splayed the book on her coffee table, turned down the radio, and said, "Here," as she reached for the wine and pie. "You ever hear of a sack?" They toted the food and wine to the kitchen counter; then she put the cheese in her freezer.

Jill moved near him and sniffed. "Did you wash your hair with that bar soap in your tub?"

"Such are the rigors of an ascetic," Maytubby said. He removed the twist tie around the cilantro, rinsed the leaves under the tap, shook them, and laid them on a chopping block. He unwrapped the pie and slid it onto a saucer from her cupboard. "I thought you were drawn to my rugged frontier simplicity."

Jill grabbed the sweating Chardonnay by its neck and held it toward him. She canted her head and gave him the stink eye.

He shrugged. "Okay, okay."

"All right, then," she said, and jabbed a corkscrew through the foil capsule. She pulled the cork, reached into her cupboard, took down two wineglasses, and poured a measure in each. She turned off the radio, started an Allen Toussaint CD, and lit her gas oven with a kitchen match.

"Why am I chopping this cilantro?" Maytubby said.

"Goes further. Loaves and fishes." Jill set a glass by the chopping block.

"So you're saying"—Maytubby took sip of wine—"it wasn't a miracle. The disciples just fed the multitude with fish flakes and tiny croutons?"

Jill picked up her glass and folded her arms. "I hadn't really thought it through."

Maytubby finished the cilantro and shoved it to the side of the board. He set his glass down and stepped to Jill's side. He kissed the nape of her neck. When she didn't unfold her arms, he said, "Trouble in Tupelo?"

"Just a little, at the end." She unfolded her arms and touched his shoulder as he took up his glass and turned to face her. "Oh, the teachers and kids loved the Eagle play. Nothing like a conga line of leaping children brandishing"—she mimed the word gently so she wouldn't spill her wine—"fake fruits and veggies."

"And the fly in the ointment?" Maytubby said.

"A parent in the parking lot when I was stowing my props in the nation van. Muscled guy wearing a pistol." Jill set down her wine and leaned on the counter. "He strolls over to me, stops, points at the nation logo on the van and says, 'I know what you're doing.'

"'So do I,' I said, and slammed the van door shut. I almost put my hands on my hips.

"'Comin' up here with your casino money and tryin' to tell our kids what they can and can't eat. Bad enough the government comes in and forces our lunch ladies to slop things on the plate our kids won't eat. My girls come home *starvin*'.'"

"I said, 'Sir, you look like you take care of yourself and eat right.' Cut the edge a little, you know. Then I said, 'I'm sure you see to it that your children do, too. But other children are on the road to diabetes if they don't learn to enjoy fruits and vegetables and ditch the honey buns.' Then I gave him a big smile and said, 'Have a good day, sir.' When I turned to go around to the driver's door, kids came rushing out of the school toward their parents' cars and school buses." Jill walked to the kitchen table and turned to face Maytubby. "Two little girls bounced toward the van, waving." Jill mimed waving. "'Hi, Daddy!' They were heavy kiddos. They hit me from both sides with big hugs and jumped up and down. The older one said, 'The Eagle play was fun, Miz Milton! Please come back!'"

"Uh-oh," Maytubby said.

"Yeah," Jill said. "I hugged them both real quick and didn't look at Daddy. I said, 'Thank you. It *was* fun.' Before I could turn around, Daddy said, 'Git away from her, girls. Git in that truck *right* now, before I give you a whuppin'.' I could see through the van windows. The girls were ducking and hangdog. Daddy's face was red. He kicked the van bumper, got in his pickup, slammed the door, and spun up gravel in reverse. Some kids squealed and ran out of his way."

Maytubby set his wine on the counter and stood up straight.

Jill rubbed her temple with her index finger and looked through the kitchen window before she looked back at Maytubby. "All the fruits and vegetables in Christendom won't help those girls."

"No."

"They made a fool of their daddy. And they'll never understand, no matter how long he lectures them or how hard he spanks them." Jill slammed her hand on the dining table. Maytubby flinched, it was so unlike her. "That prick!" Her eyes glistened. "Wearing a gun to fetch his children from school. To show them and everyone he's a big man. A man who protects his family." She crossed her arms and paced the small room, her head thrown back. She breathed deeply. "Stop me before I say, 'What's this place coming to?'"

"Be my guest," he said.

She stood quiet. The hour tolled from the First Presbyterian steeple down King's Road. "I feel like I set a trap for those girls. Even though I know it's this time and this place that snared them."

"And the prick, a creature of this time and place," Maytubby said.

"*Mmmm.*" Jill tapped the copy of *Olive Kitteridge* on the table and held it facing Maytubby.

"Speaking of," he said.

"Yeah, Olive can't believe her grown son doesn't love her . . ."

"But she admits that when he was a kid, she beat him black and blue," Maytubby said. "And that was in New England, as far from the Bible Belt as you can get."

Jill nodded and set the novel on the coffee table. She walked to Maytubby's side and leaned on the counter. He lifted her wineglass, and she shook her head. "In a minute." He set it down beside his own.

Maytubby said, "We love the curmudgeonly Olive. And pity her. I would say she didn't know any better."

"Except that our parents never spanked us," Jill said.

"No," Maytubby said.

"Or wore a sidearm to the 4-H rabbit show." Jill handed Maytubby two bell peppers and a small zucchini. "Make 'em go further." He took a sip of wine and set his glass next to the chopping board.

Jill took a jar of Hatch green chile sauce and a can of white beans from the cabinet and set them on the counter. She took the mozzarella out of the freezer, unwrapped it, pulled a flat grater from a drawer, took a hearty pull of wine, and went to work while Maytubby chopped.

"My great-aunt Lydia Maytubby sent you some pecan pie." He pointed at it with his chef's knife. "Natives."

Jill glanced at it, nodded, and looked at Maytubby. "I can tell by your face you learned something about Cy Mead."

"He drove his grandmother to Aunt Lydia's for Bible study, and he took them both to Johnson Chapel every other Sunday. Lydia was afraid we were at her house because he was in trouble."

Jill knocked cheese off the grater. "When it's worse than that," she said.

"All I could say was that his family had reported him missing. When I asked her about an allotment around Mill Creek, she said Cy had been obsessing about an allotment there—had even looked in the Dawes books at the courthouse in Tish." Maytubby sliced the zucchini lengthwise and began paring slivers. "She described Cy's car, and I showed her a picture of a 2001 Ford Focus. She identified it. Red. Hannah called Garn to see if he'd towed one the last couple days. He had. Abandoned at a low-water crossing by Ten-Acre Rock. Hannah and I searched that creek downstream and found Cy Mead's CDIB card."

Maytubby lit a burner with a kitchen match, drizzled some olive oil into an iron skillet. While the oil heated, he said, "We didn't find his license."

Jill poured a thin layer of chile sauce on the bottom of a baking dish. "You were probably lucky to find the CDIB card. But you say that about the license a little ominously."

Maytubby frowned at the skillet.

Jill stopped grating. "Oh. The bastards will have his family's address. And his family could lay claim to the allotment, too."

"Maggots," he said. "That's what Hannah calls them: 'the maggots.' And you are a step ahead, and that is why I love you." He tilted the board and slid the peppers and zucchini into the hot oil. "In addition to your virtuoso banjo frailing."

Jill finished grating the mozzarella, swept it into the bowl. "That sounds suspiciously conditional," she said, raising an eyebrow.

"Guilty," he said. He tossed the squash and peppers with a spatula. "Without a banjo, you are nothing to me."

Jill smiled. "You want to go watch the Mead house."

"Surveil." Maytubby added the white beans and some chile sauce to the skillet. "We law enforcement professionals use the term 'surveil.'"

"So you've said. What's Hannah doing tonight?"

"Surveilling the maggots' house," Maytubby said. He stirred the beans. Toussaint finessed a piano tremolo in "Viper's Drag."

"Wouldn't she tail any of the maggots who left the house?"

"She would," Maytubby said, "but more than one might leave." He turned off the burner.

Jill laid corn tortillas on the chopping block, and Maytubby spooned lines of filling onto them. She rolled the enchiladas and settled them into the baking dish. Then Maytubby poured the rest of the chile sauce over the enchiladas. She crowned the dish with mozzarella and slid it into the oven.

She set a mechanical kitchen timer for twelve minutes and held out her glass. "Sergeant Sommelier, if you will." He poured her some wine but left his glass on the counter.

"Speaking of French," he said.

"Oh, not again."

"There was this rich dude in Dicus Market tonight, from the City—I checked the plate on his new black Lincoln Navigator a little later. He was dissing the deli food. Saying the place was run by hicks."

"So you spoke French to him to show him he was wrong."

Maytubby deadpanned, "Why do I always feel like you're living my déjà vu?"

"Something might happen to my frailing thumb. Think of it as insurance."

Maytubby shook his head like a wet dog.

"Did it work?" Jill said.

"Vicky was working the deli. She played along." Maytubby ran hot water into the sink and added dish detergent and the board, bowls, and grater.

"What did the dude think of that?" She was taking dinner plates from the cabinet, utensils and cloth napkins from a drawer.

"To quote P. D. Q. Bach, I think he was really nonplussed."

Jill laughed out loud. As she set the table, she said, "Did you run the plate because power crooks drive those cars in the movies?"

"Yes." Maytubby washed the board and set it in a drainer. "It's called 'cinematic profiling.'"

The timer rang. Jill picked up potholders, opened the oven, and set the enchiladas on an iron trivet between their plates. "And what would Hannah call it?"

"'Minding the stick-outs,' I believe." Maytubby finished the grater and prep bowls and ran tap water into tumblers, which he set on the table. He left his empty wineglass on the counter.

When they sat down to dinner and the dish was cooling, Jill said, "No candle, I see. And no more wine for you. Did you bring your pecans and dried cranberries for the long night?"

"No." Maytubby forked two enchiladas onto Jill's plate. "I thought I could talk myself out of going." He plated his own enchiladas. It was late, and they ate quickly. Toussaint's piano settled behind them.

After they laid their forks on their plates, Maytubby said, "When I went to the liquor store for wine, the dude was there. He bought a case of Keystone."

Jill drank some wine. "Messes with the profile."

"Does. I hid and watched him check out. He asked the owner if he spoke French."

She laughed. "Did the owner say. 'Do I *what*'?"

"He did. I caught the dude coming out, and he said . . ."

"This is not for *me*," Jill said.

"And 'I wouldn't drink this swill.' That's when I ran his plate."

"Nichols Hills? Edmond? Deer Creek?"

"The last." Maytubby carried their plates to the sink and washed them.

Jill followed him with the baking dish. "You're still favoring that foot. You already dressed it?" She ran tap water into a coffee decanter and poured it into a drip coffeemaker, shook some ground coffee into a permanent filter, and started the machine.

"Yes," he said. He rummaged in her refrigerator, found some dried apricots and pecans they had toasted.

When it finished, Jill poured the coffee into an ancient plaid thermos, screwed down its metal flask lid and plastic red cup. Maytubby pocketed his snack and stood next to Jill at the counter. "Thanks for making coffee," he said.

"I know you have your goober teeth. You want to take the freed-man's Springfield along?" she said.

Maytubby laughed and picked up the thermos. "I'll leave the field artillery to LeeRoy." They kissed and then pressed their cheeks together. In her ear, he whispered, "I'll seize ya when I sees ya."

CHAPTER 23

Maytubby was passing Stonewall on his way to Cairo when Hannah's name lit up his cell phone on the Ford's bench seat. It was just past midnight. "Hannah," he said.

"You missed all the fun," she said.

"Red or Princess?" Maytubby's headlights swept a naked brick chimney.

"Princess. I tailed him from Chadwick Road to Tish. He crashed the red Chevy pickup through Garn's fence. Found out Mead's Focus was in there, tried to burn it up with a Molotov cocktail. Magaw was watching the lot."

"Magaw? At night?" Maytubby said.

"I'm tellin' ya. He's got a hand in this game. But it gets better. Garn busted out his fire extinguisher. Princess caught hisself on fire. Garn put him out and then hit the grass fire before it touched the Focus. Magaw and me had Princess down, but the big lug tried to rassle free. Garn blasted him in the face with the extinguisher."

"*Garn,*" Maytubby said.

"He was somethin'." Hannah coughed. "EMTs carted Princess off to Mercy after Magaw read him his rights. Katz is watching the Focus."

"*Phoo-oo!*" Maytubby said. He stopped at a traffic light in Coalgate.

"Sounds like you're drivin'," Hannah said. "I thought I'd be roustin' you out of bed with your girlfriend."

"I'm in Coalgate, going to watch the Mead house."

"Before the nonsense at Garn's," Hannah said, "I'd have called you a worrywart for doin' that."

"Who knows where Red is," Maytubby said.

"That's it. By the way, Red's name is Tim—I heard Princess call him *Timbo*. We got no driver's license or name for Princess. There was a new vehicle at the maggots' house, besides the long-hair lawyer's and the hippies' motorcycle. Black Lincoln Navigator. I saw one like it at Garn's earlier."

"Any Keystone empties in Princess's Chevy?" Maytubby dropped his column shifter into third as the lights of Coalgate fell away.

The phone was silent a few seconds. "Three," Hannah said. "Where did *that* come from?"

"The Navigator belongs to Mitchell Searcy."

"Or *that*. Shit. I already ran that plate at Chadwick Road."

"A true lawman is ever vigilant."

"Yeah, right," Hannah said.

Maytubby said, "So we know he owns the land surrounding the squatters. Rich guy like that wouldn't foul his own nest unless he had a big stake. And it's not mineral rights. No oil or gas around there. Deer-hunt land?"

"What I'm thinkin'. Maybe he brought the Echols hippies into this a long time ago," Hannah said. "Or bullied 'em."

"Either the Echolses or Searcy must have looked up the Mead homestead patent. Getting that land and killing someone doesn't seem worth the money he'd get for a deer lease. Maybe he planned to butter up his clients. I googled him. He owns an aviation company." Maytubby braked for a pack of wild dogs boiling up out of the ditch. He couldn't see their prey.

"What about Princess and Tim?" Hannah said. "Searcy was at their house. He has to know they're running drugs."

"And that they're morons. I'm getting close to the turnoff at Cairo."

"Watch out for Larry and Jerry," Hannah said before she ended the call.

A quarter mile before the Mead house, Maytubby turned off his headlights and drove slowly, by moonlight. Chat crunched under the pickup's tires. He rolled down his window. A couple of hundred yards shy of the house, he found the shade of a bois d'arc tree and killed his engine. The windows of the house were dark, its exterior washed by moonlight.

He checked his mirrors, bent forward, pulled the seat-back toward him, and lifted out his duty belt and pistol, which he laid on the bench seat. He felt above for the 20-gauge pump in its ceiling rack, leaned over, and cranked down the passenger window. The cab filled with night sounds—crickets and tree frogs, a barred owl.

Over those gentle sounds, he heard, to the west, a faint clattering. It came and went, then grew louder and constant. Like drumstick clicks in a marching band. Maytubby peered into the moonlit field. He saw juking forms. He pulled out his Maglite and shined it into the field. Two whitetail bucks were doing rut battle. They locked antlers, drove with their haunches. They rolled on the earth, backed loose, and charged again. Their tongues lolled out. After a few minutes, the larger buck, with the bigger rack, submitted, jogging slowly away. The victor stood his ground.

Maytubby switched off his flashlight. He watched the Mead house. Cy had been missing four days. The family would be anguished, clawing at nothingness. He could leap over OSBI and its forensic anthropologist. Knock on the door and tell them what he knew. Prepare them for the worst, when it was confirmed. Which might take days. If he told them, they would call the Coal County sheriff, who knew nothing and would contact Magaw or the OSBI. Back to nothingness for the Meads. And big trouble for the Lighthorse policeman who got out of line. He could play the tribal kinship card, swear the Meads to silence. A crime-novel fantasy. He checked his mirrors again and again.

If Red—Tim—or the Echolses showed up, what would they do? They wouldn't try to burn down the house and, what, shoot the family members as they tried to escape? They wouldn't break into the house and shoot everybody. Either would be ruinous for their scheme. One murder, on remote land, and an incinerated body—they might think they could hide that. Same for trying to kill LeeRoy, an old bachelor living in Bumfuck. Even torching the Focus in Garn's ramshackle lot. That might have seemed an easy expedient. Had Princess been treated at Mercy and released to the Johnston County jail? If he had called the long-haired lawyer, Fisk Bortel, the whole gang would be on alert, keeping their heads down.

At 3:40 a.m., Hannah called Maytubby and said Red Tim had threatened LeeRoy with a pistol. LeeRoy had winged him with his shotgun, and the maggot had left. She didn't know where Red was headed, but she was coming to the Mead house. He should keep an eye out for Red.

"Will do," he said.

———

A little after four, Maytubby unscrewed Jill's thermos and drank coffee, munched some roasted pecans and dried apricots. The moon had set, and the Milky Way cut across his windshield from northwest to southeast. The bois d'arc canopy obscured the overhead part. What had his grandmother called the Milky Way? Something about a dog. *Ofo* or *Ofi*. That was "dog." White dog. That was the Chickasaws' mythic white War Dog. It guided the people and protected them from enemies. Disappeared in the Mississippi River during the forced removal. *Ofi' Tohbi. Tohbi* was white. The last word came to him. *Ihina'.* "Path." *Ofi' Tohbi' Ihina'.* "The White Dog's Path." Maytubby's arms goosefleshed.

A rooster crowed at the Mead house.

Hannah texted that she was at the twins' shack, but gave no reason and said not to reply. She had been chasing Red from LeeRoy's. If Red knew where the twins had stashed his Oxy, he must be in cahoots with them. He replayed the 'Cuda chase in his mind. "What about the other'n?" Hannah had said, meaning the second of Red and Princess's pistols. The twins had kept one. "Huh," he said to himself. And thought, *Hannah's in the middle of something, too.* Then he mentally mapped the roads to the shack.

In his rearview, Maytubby saw headlights, maybe a mile behind him. If a neighbor saw his pickup parked with its light off, that would raise a flag. He started the Ford and drove beyond the house before he switched on his lights. At the first section-road intersection, he made a U-turn and drove slowly back toward the Mead house.

The headlights, which passed him exactly at the Mead house, belonged to an old Ford pickup with a cattle rack on the back. Maytubby drove to the next section line, turned around, and settled back under the bois d'arc. The Mead house had lost its moon luster. Starlit, it was a shadowy hulk.

A pack of coyotes approached, wailing and yelping in high tenor. Maytubby had read that dogs howl at sirens as a pack response. He watched the dark field to the west but couldn't see the coyotes.

At a quarter till five, a single headlight flickered in his rearview. He started the pickup, inched past the house, switched on his headlights, and again made for the section-road crossing. The vehicle was either a truck with a broken headlight or a motorcycle. When he reached the crossing, he stopped and buckled on his duty belt. Then he drove back toward the Mead house.

The single headlight was still approaching. As he neared the house, the light went out. Maytubby drove slowly with his headlights on.

The white-bearded Stan Echols braced the cycle with thin splayed legs. Maytubby could see his wife's long white hair spreading behind his torso. As the pickup drew closer, Stan squinted into its headlights, Marva tilted her head to see what was going on. Maytubby left his engine running, parked square in front of them, in the middle of the road. He took his badge wallet from his pocket and stepped out of the pickup. The cycle's engine was off.

Maytubby stood beside his pickup so as not to create a silhouette target. He watched the Echolses' hands. "Don't even think about it," he said. He briefly held out his badge in front of his left headlight, pivoted it, and put it back in his pocket. He kept his hand on the butt of his pistol. "Lighthorse Police. Mr. and Mrs. Echols, we take care of our own. As you will find out." Stan's eyes went wide, then narrowed to a squint.

A porch light flicked on at the Mead house. Maytubby registered the light but did not turn his head. He said, "I will report this threat to the Johnston County sheriff and state investigators. And I'll make sure your bond is revoked." He heard the creak of a spring door at the house, a big dog barking. Stan turned his head toward the house. Maytubby didn't have time to follow his gaze before a white chow dog scrambled into his headlights and sank its teeth into the right leg of Stan's black leather pants.

"Blanche!" a woman's voice shouted from the house.

Stan strained at his leg and shook it. The weight of the dog kept the cycle balanced, but Marva threw out her legs and toed the road anyway.

As Maytubby moved toward the snarling dog, the woman yelled, "Drop it, Blanche!" The dog released the pant leg but stood its ground, growling and barking. An elderly woman wearing a green shift and house slippers stepped into the headlights, bent, and grabbed the dog's collar. She turned the dog, still barking and writhing, and, still bent over it, pulled it to the house and through the doorframe.

Maytubby turned toward the cycle. "Turn that machine around and head back where you came from. If your friend Tim—the redhead—is waiting out there somewhere, tell him not to come here."

Suddenly, Stan Echols looked haggard. He nodded once and kick-started the cycle. He and his wife worked their legs and managed to get it headed in the opposite direction. He gunned the throttle, and they roared south.

Maytubby unbuckled his duty belt and laid it on his truck's bench seat. He shut the door softly and stood in the headlights. Dust and exhaust from the cycle swirled around him. The dog continued to bark. A light came on in the front room of the house. The screen door opened, and someone walked out, eased the screen shut, and came toward him. Between the porch light and the edges of his headlights, he could see that it was a woman. When she came into his headlights, he saw she was middle-aged, wearing a pink terry-cloth robe. Her eyes were swollen, and she crossed her arms against the chill. Maytubby stepped into the light, facing her.

"*Chokma*, ma'am. I'm Bill Maytubby. My auntie is Lydia Maytubby."

"Oh, sure. Yes." She smiled and nodded. Then she looked at the ground and her neck froze. Her hands suddenly went to her face. "You're the Lighthorse policeman. Oh, no." Her face trembled, and she held out her hands as if in supplication.

Maytubby took her left hand in his and gently grasped her elbow with his right hand. "We should go inside to talk where it's warm." She began to weep. Maytubby had to steady her gait. "Oh, Cy," she groaned.

The older woman opened the screen door. She had put on an autumn leaf print jacket over her shift. When she saw her daughter—or daughter-in-law, Maytubby didn't know—she spread her arms to embrace her. Maytubby released her and stepped back. The white chow nosed between the women's legs and whimpered.

"Lydia's nephew," the daughter sobbed into her mother's neck.

"Oh, Lord Jesus," the mother said flatly. She led her daughter to a worn corduroy couch and eased her down. The dog jumped onto the couch and laid its head against the mother's shoulder. A gas wall furnace roared to life, its innards popping.

Maytubby, trying not to limp, pulled a bentwood chair toward the couch and sat, leaning toward them, elbows on his knees. The daughter shook her head slowly against her mother's neck. The mother—his aunt Lydia's friend and Cy's grandmother—looked stoically at Maytubby. "I'm Rose Turner. This is my daughter, Linda Mead. She's Cy's mother. What can you tell us?"

Maytubby clasped his hands together. "I can't tell you anything for certain, but I have seen some evidence that Cy Mead was the victim of foul play. The State Bureau and I are investigating. We should know more very soon. And I'm sorry I can't tell you much more now. I saw the missing-persons report, and I know you have been very worried."

Rose Turner laid her hand gently on her daughter's head. "Thank you, Officer . . ."

"Bill, please."

"Thank you, Bill. Now we can be prepared." She ruffled the hair behind Blanche's ear. "Why were you on our road tonight—this morning—and who were those old people on the motorcycle?"

Maytubby cleared his throat and considered his answer. Linda pulled a Kleenex out of her robe pocket and blew her nose.

The pickup's engine muttered on the road. "I was watching your house," he said. "The people on the motorcycle—and some other people they know—they're rough folks. We think they're all connected in whatever happened to Cy." The vagueness chafed Maytubby, but he couldn't do better. "I was afraid . . ." he said.

Rose caught his eye and silently mouthed, above her daughter's head, *The allotment.*

Maytubby nodded. She had been mulling this.

Rose pursed her lips and nodded back.

"What?" Linda said.

"Nothing." Rose patted her head.

"The folks on the motorcycle won't be bothering you."

"Can I make you some coffee, Bill?" Rose said.

"Thanks. I have some in my pickup. Could you give me a good phone number in case I need to contact you?"

"Do you have a pencil and paper?" Rose said.

"You can just tell me. I remember things."

She recited her number. Maytubby stood and carried his chair back to its place. He took a business card out of his jeans pocket and laid it on an end table. "My cell number is on here. Call me if you need anything. If you're in immediate danger, call the Coal County sheriff or the Highway Patrol."

"Thank you for watching the house and for telling us what you know," Rose said.

"Yes," her daughter said without showing her face.

Maytubby opened the door and then turned back toward them. "Oh, you can tell Aunt Lydia about our talk if you want to."

Rose nodded, and he walked outside. At the verge of his pickup's headlight beams, he saw a skeletal whitetail buck rear its head, leap a fence, and trot into the brush. A Mead rooster crowed again. The sky had just begun to pale. The White Dog's Path faded.

Maytubby got in the pickup's cab, pulled to the edge of the road, and shut off his engine and lights. He got out again and stood in the road, watching and listening. He smelled brewing coffee from the Meads' house. The front door opened, and the chow walked outside. She spotted Maytubby and sat quietly on the front porch. A train blew for a crossing—Maytubby guessed Union Pacific in Stringtown, the closest town on the line.

A faint blue meteor streaked the twilight.

The Echolses may not have been killers, but they were certainly scouts. Princess was in the Tish jail. Was Red really at the twins' shack? Maytubby's toe and ribs throbbed. He leaned against the pickup's fender and lifted his sore foot, watching the dirt road.

CHAPTER 24

Maytubby had not slept for twenty-four hours.

He pulled his cell from his pants pocket and called the Light-horse Police dispatcher.

"Hey, Bill."

"Hey, Sheila. You don't work graveyard," Maytubby said.

"Burl's got the stomach flu," she said.

"Speaking of."

"Since when was Sergeant Maytubby ever sick?"

"Remind me," Maytubby said. A dusty white pickup passed on the road.

"I heard that vehicle," she said. "You're not sick at home."

"I'm sick in the country," he said. "A man can be sick anywhere."

"I was a little suspicious about Burl. I'm a lot suspicious about you."

"I'm taking a day of personal leave. I think . . ."

"Blah, blah. You have a crap ton of leave." She lowered her voice. "So, are you working on that burnt-up body over by Mill Creek? I heard Chief Fox talking about it in the hall."

"I couldn't take leave for that," Maytubby said, smiling to himself.

"Oh, shuckin's," she whispered. The line was quiet a few seconds. "You sound tired. You okay?"

"Am I *okay*? I'm at death's door."

Sheila barked a laugh. Then she said, "Sergeant Bill Maytubby, one day personal leave for heaves and trots. Chief Fox has a stack of subpoenas for you. If you're still alive in twenty-four hours."

"Thanks, Sheila."

Maytubby texted Jill: "*All is peace and joy and love in Cairo. Taking a power nap in the truck.*"

He then texted Hannah: "*Tell Magaw I ran the Echolses off from the road in front of the Mead house. He needs to get their bond revoked and jail them.*"

He stepped up into the Ford's cab and shut the door. He set his phone timer to twenty minutes, laid it on the bench seat, settled his head between the side window and the seat back, crossed his arms over his chest, and fell dead asleep.

At the alarm's first gentle beep, Maytubby bolted up, shut it off, and shook his head. A few seconds later, he saw Rose crossing in front of his pickup, carrying a small paper bag. He rolled down his window.

She handed him the bag, which was warm and greasy. "I saw in the porch light you were sleeping," she said. "Thought you might like a sausage biscuit."

"I would," he said. He plunged his hand into the bag and took out his breakfast. "How is Linda doing?"

"She's still asleep," Rose said.

Maytubby took a large bite of the biscuit, unscrewed his thermos, and washed it down with coffee.

Rose looked down the road. "You think Cy's dead because he was nosing around that allotment and somebody else wants it."

Maytubby cleared his throat.

Rose extended her hand through the open window and laid it on his shoulder. "I know, I know. You haven't finished your investigation, Bill. But do you have any idea who might've done such a thing?"

Maytubby nodded. "We have four strong suspects, maybe five. Still waiting on evidence from state investigators."

Rose patted his shoulder and withdrew her hand. "We moved the shotgun up by the front door. May the Lord bless you in your pursuit of justice."

"Thank you, Rose." He raised the sausage biscuit. "It's delicious, and I was really hungry."

Rose nodded and walked back to the house. Blanche followed her inside.

Maytubby finished the sausage biscuit and folded the sack neatly.

CHAPTER 25

In the alley behind Garn's garage, Bond slept for an hour in the front seat of her Skylark. Her head rested against the passenger window, and her boots, even with her knees bent, pushed against the passenger firewall. She awoke, starved, at 2 a.m. and squinted into the garage floodlights cutting between the wooden fence pickets.

She put her duty belt and Steiner binoculars in order on the bench seat, started the car, and drove to E-Z Mart on Main Street. When she entered the store, she woke the young clerk, who lifted his head from the counter. "Oh, hey, Hannah."

"Hi, Mark." She opened a glass freezer and corralled two sloppy joes, unwrapped them and slid them into a microwave, pushed the start button. While the carousel spun, she walked to the Bunn coffee brewer, pulled out a large Styrofoam cup, took the decanter off the warmer, and filled the cup with long-burned coffee. She turned to Mark, "Want me to start a new batch?"

He yawned and shook his head. "Naw. Won't be nobody in for two more hours. The drunks has all ate and left."

Bond nodded. She walked to the counter and paid. Mark dropped the change into a penny saucer. The microwave dinged. She yanked napkins from a dispenser and held them under the sloppy joes after she pulled them out and stacked them. She held her coffee high in a salute. "Thanks, Mark."

"You got it, Hannah." Mark bent his head to the counter.

Hannah drove west out of Tishomingo. She passed Katz, asleep in his cruiser. Before she hit the city limits, she had finished one of the sloppy joes. She crossed Pennington Creek and veered north on Oklahoma 1. She kept an eye out for the GMC, which Red Tim would be driving. When she bumped over the silica plant's rail spur, the conveyors and towers ablaze with floodlights, graveyard-shift workers' pickups nosed into the lot. When she reached the maggots' place on Chadwick Road, it was dark. She turned into the driveway. Not a single vehicle.

She retraced her route, then joined Oklahoma 7 east through the bouldered Big Rock Prairie to Butcher Pen Road to check up on LeeRoy Sickles. When she pulled into his long dirt driveway at 3:15, his porch light was on. She saw him rise from a porch chair and swing his shotgun up. She blinked her headlights and tapped her horn. He lowered his gun and peered toward her car. Before she got too close, she stopped the Skylark, opened the door, and pulled herself out.

"LeeRoy, it's Hannah!" she shouted.

He leaned the gun against the wall of his house and motioned her to come ahead.

She drove to the house, parked, and walked up the stairs onto his porch.

LeeRoy, wearing overalls and white T-shirt, put his hands behind his lower back and bent backward, stretching. "Well, Tall Drink," he said. "Yore a little late to the show." He grinned and did his marionette bounce, wiped his mouth with the back of his hand.

"Whatcha mean?" Bond said.

"Oooooh, goddamn. That GMC showed up again a few minutes ago. Short feller with a little red beard hopped out with a pistol in his hand. Reelin' drunk. I laid down on him and gave him the right barrel. Just winged 'im, I think. He got right back in the truck and drove off. The pissaint."

"Did he drop his pistol?" Bond said.

"Don't think so," Sickles said.

Bond strode down the stairs. "Gotta chase 'im," she called over her shoulder.

"Run that bastard to ground!" he shouted.

Bond opened her car door and shouted back, "We got the tall one with the mask!"

Sickles put his arms over his head and bounced his hands in a little marionette dance.

Bond scooted down Butcher Pen Road. She broke out the second sloppy joe, ate it from her right hand while she steered with her left palm. She braked for several doglegs and met the highway to Coalgate. In Clarita, she passed the Amish buggy repair shop, then headed due east. The Skylark's lifters clattered as she pushed the old car to its limits. The road was deserted. She kept an eye on the bar ditches in case Tim was seeing double and took the wrong road.

Bond called Maytubby. When he picked up, she said, "Red Tim just went after LeeRoy again. LeeRoy winged him with the cannon. I'm on Thirty-One west of Coalgate. Seat of my pants, but look out for the GMC."

"Thanks. Will do."

This was the same stretch of road where the twins Larry and Jerry, in their purple Barracuda, had passed her and Bill and run down Princess and Red Tim to rob them. She or Maytubby—she couldn't recall—had reckoned the twins overheard the maggots plotting in a country bar.

"Damn!" Bond struck the steering wheel and made the Skylark wobble. The twins had chunked only one of the maggots' pistols. Either Princess or Red Tim was two-timing his partner. Princess was in the caboose. So maybe Red Tim wasn't headed to the Mead house. Maybe he was headed to the twins' shack on Coalgate Reservoir, where they had stowed the Oxy they stole from the GMC. If he would turn on Princess, he'd turn on the twins. He would loot that shack.

She searched the long straightaway in front of her and saw

taillights a mile or so ahead. She floored the Skylark and felt it shimmy at ninety-five. Speed did not excite her. The taillights flashed and vanished left—just where the purple 'Cuda had run down the GMC on the washboard road and the twins had robbed the maggots.

Bond didn't risk a country tail on a setting-moon road to find out if the lights belonged to the GMC. She knew a shortcut to the lake. The Mead house in Cairo was only six miles away as the crow flies. If the taillights didn't belong to the GMC, and Red Tim had gone to the Meads', she could get to Maytubby in minutes.

Coalgate Reservoir was in Coal County, fifteen miles out of her jurisdiction. It was also in the Choctaw Nation, ten miles east of Maytubby's. But the tribal police were cross-deputized. If push came to shove, State Trooper Renaldo's number was on her phone.

She drank burnt coffee from the Styrofoam cup and slid it back into a hanging door holder. The shortcut turnoff was two miles. She turned on the car radio and pushed a preset button for KXFC in Coalgate, turned the volume down low. Who set the station, she didn't know or care. The hit songs meant nothing to Hannah, who had heard little music in her childhood. Maybe a foster parent's country-western radio station through a closed door.

The dirt shortcut wound between scrubby fencerows. Hannah paused briefly at an unsigned crossroads, swerved to miss a snuffling armadillo. She switched off the radio so she could remember the fork Maytubby had taken in the rutted trail to the twins' shed. He had told Larry and Jerry she was his wife. She half-smiled at that. At State Highway 3, she stopped. She needed to wait for Red to get to the shack and out of his truck.

She picked up her cell phone and considered calling Sheriff Magaw. Unthinkable, in the years she had worked for him. The business at Garn's tonight changed everything. He was in this with her and Bill. But he would be sleeping beside his wife in their comfy ranch house, his phone on silent mode. She tapped her phone's green button and waited.

A beer truck whooshed by on the highway.

"Deputy Bond," he said. No throat-clearing, no grog in his voice. In fact, he sounded pumped.

"Sheriff, the mag—the, uh, accomplice of the guy we took down at Garn's—"

"That guy has a name now," Magaw said. "Cleet Rankin. Go on."

"The other guy is a short redhead, name of Tim. He went after LeeRoy Sickles again tonight."

"Foolhardy."

"Yeah, LeeRoy winged him with the ten gauge," Bond said. "Tim left LeeRoy's. Sergeant Maytubby is watching the house where Cy Mead lives—lived—with his mother and grandmother around Cairo. I drove in that direction, but I may of seen the GMC turn toward the shack at Coalgate Reservoir I told you about, where the Larry and Jerry twins stashed the Oxy they stole from Tim and . . ."

"Cleet Rankin," Magaw said.

"That guy," Bond said. "I'm going to the shack."

"You're off duty, Hannah, I know. But you're outside the county. Want me to call Sheriff Deane in Coalgate?"

Hannah shook her head. "And roust a gaggle of Katzes and Ephs out here? No thanks."

Magaw laughed. "I wash my hands."

"Later," Hannah said, and ended the call.

She drove down the highway to the lake turnoff and followed the dwindling dirt road, well past the last house driveway so as not to rouse folks. She found a pasture entrance with a gap gate, pulled into it, and turned off her ignition. The moon was down now, but starlight would do, once her eyes adjusted. She considered buckling on her duty belt but decided to slip out her Maglite and leave the belt in the car. She had not come for an arrest or a showdown—just to see what Red Tim was up to.

She slid the Maglite in her back pocket, snugged her small old cell phone in the top of her right boot in case she got in a jam. She locked her car, laid her keys and wallet on the top of the rear driver's-side tire.

Bond slid the top wire over the gap post, stepped over the bottom wire, and dropped the top wire back in place. The pasture was native grass, so she cut across it easily, striding toward the shack. A rooster crowed in the distance. She couldn't hear the highway, only her boots crunching the grass.

There was no fence gate on the stretch nearest the shack, so she stepped on the bottom strand of barbed wire and lifted the middle one with her hand. She was too tall to bend through the gap, so she rolled through it, ripping a leg of her jeans. Her landing made some noise, so she lay there, listening.

She got on her hands and knees and pushed herself upright. The pasture ended at the fence. Bond peered into a dark stand of blackjack oaks. She pulled the cell from her boot and texted Maytubby: *At the twins shack. Dont reply.* The cell went back in her boot. Now she walked slowly, setting her boots down gently on acorns and deadwood, extending her left hand to feel for branches and trunks. Her right hand instinctively touched her thigh for the absent holster. Best guess, the shack was two hundred yards to her north.

Every few yards, Bond halted—watched and listened. Well into the blackjacks, she heard a distant engine. It grew only a bit louder—closer—but remained muffled. Could be the twins' Barracuda. Might be a rancher's pickup. She walked some more and stopped. On the road, near where she had left the Buick, a car door opened and, a few seconds later, closed. Not slammed. An older vehicle, because there was no warning chime. Larry or Jerry getting out to stand watch?

Through the blackjacks, a bright blue light danced, went dark, then danced again. Hannah assumed the light was at the shack. To keep behind the person with the light, she turned to her right, toward the rutted drive. The engine approached the Y intersection, its throaty idle cycling. Hannah saw no lights. She stopped before she broke into the road clearing. The vehicle's undercarriage *shushed* the grass between the ruts. She caught a whiff of cigarette smoke and men's cologne.

A few seconds later, the Barracuda's bulk crept past her. A cigarette tip glowed from the driver's seat. Then it arced over the car into the woods on the opposite side. Hannah could barely make the car. Its dash display faintly lit the driver's face.

She waited until the 'Cuda's brake lights glowed on the blackjack leaves and the engine fell silent. Then she paralleled the rutted trail toward the shack while staying in the woods. The 'Cuda's dome light briefly appeared before she heard the car door shut. Hannah missed her Steiners, which would have been a ball and chain. She briefly envied Maytubby his little field glasses.

She could hear a soft voice, then a loud drunken one: "Heyyy, dude!" Timbo.

"Shut up!" somebody hoarsely whisper-shouted. Larry or Jerry.

Hannah closed on the shack. Now she could dimly make out the old house foundation and hand pump. And the dim outline of a large pickup. A second firefly light joined the first. They converged at a point on the low center of the shed—likely the padlock she and Maytubby had seen. The flitting phone lights strobed the shack door opening, then disappeared inside.

Hannah listened to whispers but needed to be closer. Before she took a step, she heard a rustle far behind her. She turned, watched, listened. Maybe a possum or a skunk. A dozen more steps. Now she could see lights playing inside the shed and hear the crinkling of plastic bags and what sounded like those Mexican gourd things with rocks inside. Pill bottles. With everyone inside the shack, she stepped onto the road clearing, where she could walk silently.

A few steps, then a cold jab at the base of her skull. "Shit," she whispered. Her curiosity about the shack had rendered her deaf.

"*Yeah* shit," a man's high voice stage-whispered. The cool steel burrowed deeper into her neck. "Keep walkin'. I like to shoot dogs, 'specially big dogs." He frisked her quickly so she couldn't catch his free hand. She turned her head to blunt the stench of his cologne.

Bond let her arms fall at her sides as she trudged toward the shed. The voices inside grew more distinct. When Bond and her captor neared the door, he said aloud, though not shouting, "We got comp'ny, boys."

Just inside the door, Bond was dazzled by two blue cell phone lights. Her captor stepped quickly around her, standing beside the other two lights. The shadow of his pistol danced on the wall.

"I'll be fucked," Tim shouted.

"Not so loud!" Larry or Jerry.

"It's the *sow*!" Tim hissed.

"What?"

"*Who?*"

"Did you see a old white Buick out on that road?" Tim said.

"Yeah. That's why I let Jerry out. See if you had a visitor."

"She must of followed me here," Tim said.

"You *know* this giant dyke?" It was Larry's voice. "She put that bird shot in your butt?"

"Fuck no," Tim said. "She was parked by the Chadwick Road place. Me and Cleet thought there was neckers in her car and wanted to have a little fun. When we saw it was just her, we roughed her up and trashed her clunker."

There was a beat of silence. Someone cleared his throat. When the twins didn't question Timbo, Bond understood they owed him. It made sense. He was taking a bigger cut of the haul than he would have gotten from Princess. They had to settle for what Timbo brought them. His mess was just tough titty the twins would have to suck.

"Keep the lights in her eyes," Larry said. "We've got guns on you, woman. Brother, take off your shirt, rip off your sleeves. Blindfold her, gag her, and bind her hands behind her back."

Bond shut her eyes against the lights. She heard Jerry lay his pistol on the concrete floor, shuck his shirt, and tear off his sleeves. He must have been wearing sneakers, because she didn't hear him approach. She did smell his cologne and tobacco breath. She crossed her hands in front because they were dumbasses. He encircled her wrists with the sleeve and stopped. They *were* dumb as rocks. "Well, shit," he said. Then she heard more tearing. He was a little bastard, had to rip his sleeves longways to reach around her thick wrists.

When he had enough cloth to do the work, he made her pay,

cinching the second loop, between her wrists, with a fierce jerk before he tied it off. Bond gritted her teeth but made no sound. Jerry looped the second sleeve over her head. "Fuck!" he said, and snapped it back. Again she heard him ripping. She thought she heard Tim laughing.

Jerry gagged and blindfolded her. Bond heard him straining at the blindfold, likely on his toes. Tim brayed.

"Get her car keys," Larry said.

Tim snorted, "I don't think he can reach that high."

"I frisked her," Jerry said. "She ain't got nothin' in her pockets."

"Her junker is so old she prob'ly has to, uh . . . whatever," Tim said.

"Hot-wire it," Larry said.

"Yeah," Tim said.

Bond knew that the twins wanted to know why she was there. But Tim held all the cards, and he was too drunk to care. Tim might have killed Cy Mead. This early morning, she feared the twins more.

Through her closed eyelids and Jerry's shirt, a new darkness. The men had either turned off their cell flashlights or turned them away. Batteries had to be low. Bond heard them whispering, pacing the slab floor. She bit into the gag and chewed it like breakfast steak. They could see her hands and blindfold, so she left those for later.

"Used to be bailin' wire in these old barns," Tim said aloud. "We could wire her feet and put her outside."

"Shhhh."

"Larry, we still got *your* shirt," Tim said.

Bond heard shoes scuffing the concrete. The twins were pissed. She chewed furiously.

"Whatchu say, Larry?" Tim said.

Larry said nothing. She heard some hard breathing, faint rustling. Some footsteps, then she smelled cologne and felt someone tying her ankles. "Fucker," he muttered. When he was done, he yanked the knot toward him and thieved her balance. She fell straight back. When her skull hit the slab, she saw sparkles but did not pass out.

Bond let her body go limp, her head loll to the side. She forced herself not to swallow the shreds of Jerry's shirt at the back of her throat.

"Way to go, Larry," Tim said. "It's gonna take all three of us to drag Bigfoot outside."

"Why don't we just shoot her and throw her in your pickup," Larry said. "You can dump her in Caney Creek."

Tim didn't answer right away. A cigarette lighter clicked. "She ain't seen you two," he finally said. "Or any of this crap. I don't even know why she come to be here." He suddenly sounded tired, almost mournful.

The twins said nothing, which told Bond they didn't recognize her as Maytubby's pretend wife from her earlier visit to the shack.

"Seems to me," Tim continued, "you fellers get in enough scrapes as it is. Why'd you want to get mixed up in a killin'? This bull heifer ain't worth it. Now, let's drag her outside and do our chores."

Bond felt many hands on her ankles. Grunts and curses as the men strained to pull her over the concrete floor. They managed only a couple of yards with each effort, pausing to catch their breath and whisper oaths. She wondered if her phone would get jarred loose. At last, her pelvis, then her skull, grated over the floor lip. They dragged Bond many yards away from the shack. The grass and dead leaves cushioned the rising knot at the base of her skull.

"Okay, let's get to work," Tim said. "'Bout ready to get light." Bond heard footsteps moving away. But she smelled cologne and cigarette breath, felt the heat of another body. When the other footsteps had receded, she heard leaves crunching near her, then the small metallic click of a pistol's safety being thumbed off. She lay perfectly still, awaiting the kill shot.

CHAPTER 26

Maytubby started his pickup, made a three-point U-turn, and headed back to the Coalgate highway. Hannah had told him not to reply to her last text. So she was surveilling. And she'd been incommunicado for too long.

As the Ford jolted over the washboard road, he called Trooper Renaldo.

Jake answered at once. "Hey, Bill, what's up?"

"Where are you right now?"

"Just finished the paperwork from a DUI fatality on Seventy-Five in Lehigh. About to go off shift."

"Not sure Hannah's in trouble," Maytubby said, "but I could use backup just south of Coalgate Reservoir. You're six miles south; I'm eight east and closing. Meet me at the Coalgate Reservoir sign on State Three. I'll lead you from there."

"Will do," Renaldo said.

CHAPTER 27

Bond felt the man's hot breath, his face nearing hers. She waited until he stopped breathing, then another second, then jerked her head to the side. The shot deafened her left ear and thrummed in her head. She gritted her teeth and lay still, her good ear still free of the ground.

"*Fuck . . . fuck!*" Larry howled. She heard a commotion on the grass and leaves just before a fierce pain scalded her left temple. Then a crash on the dead branches, voices and rushing footsteps from the shack.

"You stupid *cunt!*" Larry said through his teeth. Three more quick shots from his pistol. Bond heard the rounds thudding into the earth around her. Larry gagged.

Bond felt blood pooling on the collar of her shirt. Through her blindfold, she saw blurs of moving light. "What the fuck, Larry?" Tim said. "People *live* out here." The footsteps stopped. "Did you shoot her?"

The light disappeared.

"I shot my *foot*! Got *damn* it hurts." Larry's voice quavered. "Help me up!"

Bond heard rustling and grunts.

"You *did* shoot her," Tim said. "She's bleedin' like a stuck hog. That makes two of you. Jerry, get his other arm 'round your neck." Larry whimpered and sucked air through his teeth.

Bond heard footfalls near her head. Tim said, "You shoulda practiced with my partner's fancy SIG first." The footsteps and voices grew fainter. "*And* not acted a fool. Now we're gonna have to . . ." Tim's voice faded out.

Bond lay still until the shack door closed. She could hear in one ear; she could reason and move her limbs. So the round had not struck her brain. She lifted her arms and pushed up the blindfold, set her teeth into the knot around her wrists. Instead of fighting the knot, she tugged at strands until one pulled loose, then another. Soon her hands were free. She grabbed a fistful of the maggot's sleeve and pressed it hard against her left ear. When the rag was soaked, she found the discarded blindfold, pressed that against her ear, and dropped her head against the ground to hold the compress in place. Then she bent her knees behind her and worked blind at the hobble. Her fingers were cold and stiff. She paused briefly to flex them, then went at the knot again, careful not to cinch it. From the shack, she heard Larry's faint cries and some jostling. The barest blue of twilight appeared on the fallen blackjack leaves.

The hobble was damned stubborn. She left it alone, fished the phone out of her boot, called Maytubby, and pressed the phone to her good ear.

CHAPTER 28

Maytubby's high beams lit Jake Renaldo's Oklahoma Highway Patrol cruiser parked on the shoulder of State 3 at the reservoir turnoff. Maytubby steered his pickup onto the grass beside the shoulder and rolled down his window. Jake lowered his passenger window. "Tell me, Bill."

"Follow me," Maytubby said. "Enough blue in the sky, I think we can do this without headlights. Less than a mile. This road's the only way in or out."

"Lead on," Renaldo said.

Maytubby made out the road but drove slowly. The few houses along the way were bathed in yellow sodium yard light. All their windows were dark. But as he neared the Y, he noticed a couple of people standing on their front steps. Something had roused them. He accelerated.

Soon he saw Hannah's white Skylark, pale indigo just before dawn, parked at a ranch drive. As Maytubby passed it, his phone hummed.

He accepted the call but waited to be sure nobody else had his partner's phone.

"Bill," she rasped.

"Yeah. Jake and I are almost to the Y."

"They hog-tied me and dragged me out northeast of the shed. Larry shot my ear and his own damn foot. They're all in the shed. I'll get this hobble off pretty quick." She ended the call.

Maytubby veered left at the Y and watched Renaldo follow. A few dozen yards toward the shack, Maytubby braked, turned his truck sharply to the right, and parked, blocking half the trail. Renaldo inched behind the Ford, turned his cruiser sharply left, and blocked the other half of the trail. They turned off their vehicles.

Maytubby buckled on his duty belt and took down his 20-gauge pump from its ceiling rack. He chambered a round, which left three in the magazine.

He met Jake in the trail. Renaldo wore his duty belt and pistol, carried his regulation pump 12 gauge. Maytubby said, "I got a gimp foot." He managed a slow jog up the road with Jake beside him. Maytubby spoke softly. "Hannah's been tied up and shot in the ear—not seriously. She's in the woods just to our right. You can just see the shack at the end of the trail, likely our black GMC pickup, and an old purple Barracuda. Three armed men in the shack, with a big haul of Oxy from the pharmacy break-ins you know about."

They walked in parallel ruts, Maytubby favoring his foot. When the vehicles and shack appeared in the short distance, they slowed and moved out of their ruts toward the brush line on the right side of the trail.

Maytubby and Renaldo stepped slowly, scanning the woods for Hannah. When they found her just inside a blackjack thicket, Maytubby pulled a pocketknife from his jeans and cut her hobble. She stood at once, cast away her bloody compress, then bent down, wadded up the hobble, and jammed it in her jeans pocket.

"Give me a gun," she whispered to Maytubby.

He pulled his pistol from the duty belt.

"I'm fixin' to get it sticky," Hannah whispered. She wiped her hands on her jeans. Maytubby held the pistol close to his face to check the safety, then laid the pistol grip in her right hand. He knew that though she carried the old Model 10 revolver, she had trained with his model of Beretta.

The three knelt and huddled in the woods. Maytubby whispered, "Jake and I blocked the road with the Ford and his cruiser."

Lights darted from the shack. Indistinct voices, trunks or tailgates being opened. One steady dome light appeared.

"Let 'em start loadin' the stuff," Hannah said. "Then I'll holler in pain and see if we can't get one of the turd knockers to come over and try to shoot me again."

"On your count," Renaldo said.

As dawn approached, the trio could plainly see two men carrying black plastic garbage bags out of the shack, tossing them alternately in the 'Cuda trunk and the GMC pickup bed.

Hannah waited until both men were outside the shack, at the lowered tailgate of the GMC. "Three, two, one," Hannah said. Then she laid the Beretta's barrel crosswise like a bridle bit in her teeth and belted a feral cry.

The men froze. Then they backed away from the pickup and fumbled for their pistols. Hannah heard Larry moaning in the shack. In the fresh light, she could distinguish Tim and Jerry. Tim was mostly sober by now, no longer shouting. She heard him muttering to Jerry, who raised his pistol and began walking slowly toward the woods where Larry had left her.

"I'll bait 'im," Hannah whispered. She pulled her hobble from her pocket and handed it to Maytubby. "Gag," she said softly but so Renaldo could hear. She laid the Beretta on the ground and then lay down as gently as she could, the pistol handy. To Renaldo she said, "Drop back and fall in behind the goober. His name is Jerry."

Jake stepped back some paces. Maytubby moved behind a blackjack trunk near her.

Bond turned her head toward the approaching man and squinted.

Jerry lowered his pistol to his waist as he stepped off the trail rut. He paused to listen before he took a few more steps, moving the gun left and right as he entered the shadows of the blackjack stand.

Hannah saw him find her with his eyes. He stopped twenty yards away and pointed the pistol at her. Then he took a dozen more steps.

"Hi, Jerry," Renaldo stage-whispered.

Jerry spun to his left. Renaldo hit him in the chin with the stock of his shotgun. Jerry dropped his pistol and reeled backward. Maytubby forced the gag in his mouth, rolled him facedown, and bound his wrists with plastic handcuffs from his duty belt. Bond jammed the Beretta against the base of Jerry's skull and whispered in his ear. "Not a peep. Your sorry brother shot off my ear, and I'll do the same to you. You hear?"

Jerry nodded furiously.

Bond, Maytubby, and Jake knelt in the leaves and watched Tim pace behind the GMC. They heard Larry scream, "Get me to a fucking hospital!"

"Look!" Maytubby whispered. He pointed up at the trees. The highest leaves caught red and blue strobes. "The porch folks."

"Hold on," Jake said. He fiddled with his vibrating shoulder mike and whispered into it, "Tell the Coal deputies to shut off their overheads and stand by at the white Buick parked on the road. Tell Coal County EMA to send an ambulance—no siren or lights. Renaldo out."

Tim stopped pacing. He looked toward the shack and then back toward the trail. He muttered something, then rushed back into the shack. He emerged with a fat garbage bag in each hand, tossed the bags in the back of the GMC. He jogged to the open trunk of the Barracuda, plucked out two bags, carried them to the bed of the GMC, and hurled them in.

"Go to the cruiser," Maytubby said. "I'm going to the 'Cuda."

Jake and Bond hustled up the trail. Maytubby managed a lame jog toward the shack. He heard Larry's outraged shouting, his gagged twin's muffled cries.

Tim jumped into the GMC cab, revved its engine, rammed the Barracuda's right rear fender, plowed the car aside, and gained the ruts. Maytubby saw the Jimmy's headlights flood the trail. He checked the safety on his shotgun with his finger before he opened the 'Cuda's driver door and slid the gun's barrel onto the passenger floorboard, settled the stock into the seat. He stomped the clutch, ignited the mammoth eight, and yanked the pistol-grip shifter into reverse. There was no time to about-face. He threw his right arm over the passenger seat, twisted his body so he could see out the rear window, plunged the accelerator, and popped the clutch.

The car shuddered and bucked as he guided it into the ruts. The reverse lamps, aided by twilight, lit the trail; the undercarriage thumped. Soon he saw the GMC's brake lights flash. Its headlights illuminated the cruiser and his old Ford, the heads of Jake and Hannah just above the cruiser's hood. Maytubby came almost against the GMC's tailgate before he shifted into neutral, slammed the brakes, and spun the 'Cuda's steering wheel hard left. The car slewed perpendicular to the tailgate, blocking the trail back to the shack. Maytubby killed the engine, opened the door, and pulled his shotgun out after him.

Maytubby crouched, raised his pump, and duckwalked along the pickup's bed. The driver's-side mirror caught the GMC's reverse lights. Tim hit his accelerator. The truck jammed against the muscle car. But Tim did not seem to notice. He gunned his engine. The truck jostled the 'Cuda but did not move it. The truck's spinning wheels geysered sand into the dawn light.

The racket was good cover. Maytubby laid his shotgun on the ground, took his hand away from it, and went prone. He crawled to the back edge of the driver's door, rolled onto his back, and elbowed his way under the bottom sill. In the cab, Tim raged and pounded the steering wheel. The sweet stench of exhaust swept over Maytubby as he waited for Tim to make his move.

CHAPTER 29

The rant ceased; the pickup's engine died. Tim left his headlights on—to blind whoever was behind the cruiser and the old Ford, and to see them clearly himself. Maytubby heard him bumping the door, thrashing in his seat. Then a long silence. Was he organizing magazines for his pistol?

Maytubby could hear the distant engines of Coal County deputies on the road at Hannah's Skylark. Then another far-off rooster. With every minute, daylight was eroding Tim's advantage. Would he tumble out of the cab and make a run for the woods, or step out slowly and use the pickup's door as a shield so he could open fire on Jake and Hannah?

Maytubby didn't have to wait for his answer. Tim banged the door open and fired two wild shots through its brand-new window glass before Maytubby grabbed his left foot and wrenched it violently. Tim grunted. He fired a third shot into the ground as he pitched facedown in the rut.

"Don't shoot!" Maytubby shouted toward the blockade. He scrambled onto Tim's back, pried the pistol free, and yanked Tim's right arm behind his back. For good measure, he pulled that arm far up toward Tim's neck until he cried out.

"He's down!" Maytubby yelled. "Come in! I need cuffs!"

Tim got one knee beneath him before Hannah dropped on his legs. Renaldo cuffed him.

CHAPTER 30

It was full daylight when Renaldo, from his shoulder mike, summoned the Coal County deputies and the ambulance. He and Bond dragged Tim by his armpits to the GMC, sat him up against its front fender. As a clamor approached from the reservoir road, Tim studied his captors. Renaldo soon turned and walked toward his cruiser. Tim narrowed his red-rimmed eyes. Then his mouth went slack. He shook his head. "I'll be a sum*bitch*. The drunk Indian and the bigfoot sow." He closed his eyes and let his head fall back on the fender. Then he chortled. "Fuck me," he said.

Bond guarded Tim with the Beretta while Maytubby retrieved his shotgun and limped to his pickup. He ejected all the gun's shells and stowed it in the overhead rack. He and Renaldo backed out of the track at the same time. They parked in the small clearings at the edge of the woods.

Renaldo raised an open palm to stop the first Coal County cruiser as he walked over the ruts to Maytubby, who had gotten out of his truck. "Bill, I'll direct traffic here. I'll take care of Tim and call OSBI. Hannah . . ."

Maytubby said, "I know. I'll drive her to Coal County General."

"If she'll let you." Jake smiled. He turned, jogged past the first cruiser to the ambulance.

Maytubby limped gamely to Bond's side. "The Coal deputies—"

"Ha!" Bond said. "Eph and Katz incoming."

"Jake's going to put one in charge of Tim here," Maytubby said. "I'm taking you to the ER in Coalgate."

Bond swept her left hand above her mangled ear. "This is nothin'. I'll go home and warsh it off."

"Hannah, you're still bleeding. Your shirt and pants are soaked in blood. You need stitches."

Bond touched her ear and inspected her index finger. "Well, shit," she said.

A jug-eared deputy who looked to Maytubby like an adolescent bounded to Bond's side, panting. He assumed the isosceles stance— legs spread apart, arms extended, pistol in two hands—and aimed at Tim. Tim rolled his eyes and snorted.

"Point that at the ground," Bond told him. "And make sure your safety's on."

She turned her head to Maytubby and whispered, "See? Katz."

She handed the Beretta to her partner, who holstered it. They walked to Maytubby's pickup. When they were seated, Maytubby opened his glove compartment and ferreted out some paper napkins. He handed them to Bond, who pressed them against her left ear. He drove past the ambulance, another Coal cruiser, and a Choctaw Lighthorse cruiser before gaining the dirt road. When they neared Bond's Skylark, there were two more cruisers, parked on opposite shoulders. Two men, neither in uniform, stood together in the middle of the road.

"I be damned. That's Magaw," Bond said.

"And I think he's talking to Sheriff Deane."

The men edged to the right shoulder. As Maytubby neared them, Bond rolled down her window with her free hand. The pickup rolled to a stop.

Magaw stepped to Bond's window. "Hannah! Thank the Lord

you're still among the living." He moved his head inside the window. "You're wounded."

"Bill's makin' me go for *stitches*." She curled her lips in a mock smile. "That Larry guy is worse off than me. Shot his foot 'stead of my head. We'll just beat him to the hospital. I hope he has to wait. The maggot. We also got Jerry and Tim hog-tied. And all their drugs. Why're you here?"

"That pin you sent to my phone. I waited in Stonewall until I heard all the radio chatter." Magaw looked past Bond. "Bill, get her to a doctor, pronto."

Maytubby bent forward and said, "Coal County ER." He saluted Magaw and popped the Ford's clutch.

CHAPTER 31

Maytubby sat beside a plastic philodendron in the Coal County ER. He pulled his cell from his jeans to call Jill. A gurney burst through the doors, followed by a huffing, flushed EMT and a deputy. Larry's face was a pallid grimace. The sheet tented over his wounded foot was saturated with blood. As the gurney rolled past, Maytubby said, "Hi, Larry." Then the gurney bumped through a second pair of doors.

Maytubby called Jill.

"You still in Canaan's land?" she said.

"If Coalgate is within its borders, yeah."

"It's not," Jill said. "So you're not at the Meads' house. That's in Cairo."

"I'm in the Coal County ER. Hannah got shot in the outer ear. The helix, if memory serves. She's getting stitches."

"Damn. Poor Hannah." She was silent for a beat. "'*Helix*,' though? Sounds suspiciously like your 'great toe.' Now tell me about the other guy I shoulda' seen."

Maytubby smiled. "Hannah was on the ground. He was aiming at her head. He stepped too close and shot himself in the foot. We just beat his ambulance to the ER. Hannah was gloating about making him wait."

"Where was she when this happened? Were you there, too?"

"A drug cache shack by Coalgate Reservoir. One of the maggots involved in the Mead killing cut out his buddy and teamed up with some drifters living in Coalgate. Twins named Larry and Jerry. When Hannah went quiet, I called in Jake Renaldo and we moved on the shack. Hannah was waylaid by Larry, bound and gagged."

"Not for long," Jill said. "Even though she was shot."

"No."

"And the Meads?"

Back in the ER, Larry howled like an enraged toddler.

"Was that Larry?" Jill said.

"Yes. Back to Cairo. The old hippie couple, the Echolses, showed up at the Mead house on their motorcycle. I ran them off. I also broke protocol and told Cy's mother and grandmother as much as I could . . ."

"Did you employ the phrase 'victim of foul play' in some weird conditional way?"

"What was it you said about horning in on my déjà vu?" Maytubby said. "Insurance on your frailing thumb?"

"And don't you forget it."

"Where does your nation's duty take you this crisp autumn morning?" Maytubby said.

"First, Sergeant, give me the skinny on the shack face-off."

"Thanks to Hannah's guile, we captured all three miscreants and their stash of thieved Oxy. Hannah's . . ."

"Helix," Jill said.

"Yeah, that—and Larry's foot—were the only injuries. Jake, the Coal County deputies, and the Choctaw Lighthorse are sorting things out. OSBI later."

"Hannah's not going to like that last part," Jill said. "It's going to be that Scrooby guy."

"She won't. But her boss, Sheriff Magaw, showed up at the crime scene this morning. He's on her side in this one."

"Good," Jill said.

"So, back to this crisp autumn morning," Maytubby said.

"I was called in as a sub to oversee loading the nation's mobile grocery truck," Jill said. "By 'oversee,' I mean loading cases of canned goods and cereal from the warehouse onto dollies and pushing them up a ramp to the box truck's liftgate."

"How many tons?" Maytubby said.

"Six," Jill said. "Ten pallets."

"And how many in your crew?"

"*Crew*? Two. Me and a guy I've never seen before," Jill said.

"So, what, five hours?"

"Give or take."

"Dr. Milton, stevedore."

"We have to get food to the people. But I evened the score. Jeans and socks and sneakers," Jill said. Someone hollered in the background.

"No skirt, no pantyhose," Maytubby said.

"Not on your life. Let 'em try to write me up. I know Hannah is tough as nails, but you'll stand by her. I gotta push this dolly." Jill ended the call.

CHAPTER 32

When Bond strode into the waiting room in the early afternoon, Maytubby scrambled up and limped to her. A man in aqua scrubs held her elbow until Bond yanked it away. The man frowned and looked at Maytubby. A dark bruise spanned the left half of Bond's face, and her ear was covered by a mass of gauze and tape.

The man said to Maytubby, "She wouldn't accept pain meds, even for the stitches."

"Let's get outta here," Bond said.

To the man in scrubs, Maytubby said, "I got it. Thank you."

Bond beat Maytubby to the door.

When they were seated in Maytubby's pickup, Hannah said, "Magaw called me when they were workin' on my ear. He told me Scrooby wanted to talk to you and me at the drug shack soon as I was done here."

"Considerate fellow, Scrooby." Maytubby started the Ford and pulled out of the hospital lot.

"I hope he stopped in Ada for grub. He's pure shit-ass when he's hungry. Only half when he ain't."

Maytubby drove west on State 3. Hannah said, "I still got some Slim Jims in my car. I guess you been eatin' rabbit food."

"Cy Mead's grandma gave me a sausage biscuit early this morning," Maytubby said.

Hannah faced him and raised a bruised eyebrow. "So you waited till she was gone and th'ew it out the window. Or did you save it for me?"

Maytubby got tickled and started laughing, which stung his ribs.

Hannah snorted. "Ow!" she said, and raised a hand to her ear. "Look at us. Too gimp to laugh. Stop at the Buick for my Slim Jims." She stared out the windshield. "And you ain't gettin' any."

Maytubby laughed again and held his side.

He had to park just shy of the Buick because the road was jammed with cruisers. Scrooby's OSBI Charger sat empty behind Hannah's car.

"Him all over," Hannah said. She rolled out of the Ford cab as Maytubby limped to the Skylark. She shouted, "Keys and wallet on top of the rear driver's tire. Brang me the wallet, too. The Slim Jims—"

Maytubby raised his right hand to signal that he knew where to find them.

When he returned, he handed keys, wallet, and three Slim Jims to Hannah. He waited a few seconds for her to peel off the wrapping, drop it on the ground, and devour the Slim Jims. When she turned her head toward the shack, Maytubby snatched up the plastic wrappers and put them in his pocket.

"I heard that," she said.

Then they ducked under the crime scene festoon and trod the fallen blackjack leaves toward the shack.

CHAPTER 33

Bond and Maytubby walked into the dim light of the shed. Pencil shafts of light through holes in the tin roof made bright ovals on the bare concrete floor. Agent Scrooby, wearing a black OSBI jacket, sat on an upturned bucket. He leaned over a makeshift cable-spool table and bit lustily into a Texas-toast sandwich. Hannah watched barbecue sauce ooze between slices of bacon and brisket onto a stack of fries piled on a splayed to-go sack. Hannah and Maytubby halted. She made eye contact with Sheriff Magaw, who nodded. They all knew better than to get between Scrooby and his feed.

There were several tagged evidence sacks on the spool table. Along the walls of the shack stood Trooper Renaldo, Coal County Sheriff Deane, a few deputies, and the chief of the Choctaw Lighthorse Police. Scrooby noted the arrival of Bond and Maytubby with a brief side-eye, then closed his eyes in an ecstasy of appetite. He seemed oblivious to the theater. He chewed loudly, wheezing through his nose.

When he had finished his sandwich, he mopped up barbecue sauce with the fries. He wiped his mouth with a paper napkin, dropped it onto the blotched sack, wadded up all the paper, and set it aside.

Bond whispered to Maytubby, "Here comes the pissed blow."

Scrooby obliged. He did not seem inclined to rise, so the sheriffs,

186 · BY KRIS LACKEY

deputies, and Choctaw Lighthorse chief shuffled into a semicircle in front of him. Maytubby and Bond stood still. He could see them just fine.

"We are in Coal County," Scrooby said. "Sheriff Beale, Trooper Renaldo, and the Choctaw Lighthorsemen are within their jurisdictions." He cleared his throat and silently belched. "Sergeant Maytubby, Deputy Bond, and Sheriff Magaw are not." He looked at Bond, paused, and wrinkled his nose. "Hannah, you look like death warmed over." He shook his head. Then he blew.

Sheriff Deane said, "Agent Scrooby, Sheriff Magaw is welcome here. He was concerned for the welfare of his deputy."

Scrooby raised an eyebrow and knitted his fingers. He leaned back on his bucket a little too far, lurched forward to catch his balance. He regained his composure, bent over the spool, and blew again. Then he nodded dismissively. "All right, but what the hell were *his deputy* and Sergeant Maytubby doing here in the first place?" He glared at Bond and Maytubby. His face was flushed. "My agency is engaged in a full investigation of the murder in Mill Creek. The prime suspects, Stan and Marva Echols, have been charged with possession of Schedule Two narcotics, with intent to distribute. OSBI was summoned by Sheriff Magaw to bring its considerable resources to bear on this case. And now all this"—he swept his hand toward the road—"idiotic mess. I've got a double homicide in Owasso, and this is wasting our time."

Bond exhaled through her nose.

Benny Magaw said, "They've been hard at work. Let them explain, Dan."

"Oh, I see," Scrooby turned on Magaw. "And the State Bureau of Investigation has been asleep at the wheel."

"That's not what I said, Dan," Magaw said softly.

"Deputy Bond, Sergeant Maytubby," Scrooby barked. "Who goes first?"

Bond said, "The redhead, Tim—"

Magaw said, "We have his name, Hannah. Timothy Fletcher."

Bond nodded. "Red tried to kill LeeRoy Sickles last night, and—"

"That hillbilly with the big shotgun?" Scrooby smirked.

Bond ignored him. "He was the second one to try that, after Princess—"

"*Princess?*" Scrooby gaped and shook his head.

"Cleet Rankin, Dan," Magaw said. "The guy Bond and I took down in Tish when he tried to firebomb the Focus to destroy evidence. Your agents know he wore a princess mask when he went after Sickles on Butcher Pen Road."

Scrooby blew. "Yeah, yeah."

Bond said, "I think Red's got some of LeeRoy's bird shot in his heinie. Anyway, I knew he was headed this way, because he cut out his partner, Princess, and joined up with the twins, Larry and Jerry. The ones you-all got along with Red today." Scrooby threw up his hands and started to speak. Bond said, "This won't make a lick of sense until we back up and tell the first part. Bill?"

Maytubby said, "The murder victim found in the charcoal kiln is likely Cy Mead, who lived with his mother and grandmother a few miles from here, in Cairo. You can find the date he was reported missing in the NamUs database. Cy had discovered that his ancestor, Augustus Mead, held a homestead patent for the land where the Echolses are now living. Deputy Bond confirmed this with a landman."

"Landman woman," Hannah said.

"I stand corrected," Maytubby said. "It appears that Stan and Marva Echols are squatters. According to LeeRoy Sickles, who often hunts squirrels on the land, they have been there for many years. If they stay on that land fifteen years, they can claim it. Deputy Bond's landman woman also discovered that the land adjoining the patent grant on three sides is owned by a wealthy suburban Oklahoma City man named Mitchell Searcy."

Scrooby raked his hair and blew. Cattle bawled in the pasture behind the shed. Magaw caught Hannah's eye and raised a conspiratorial eyebrow.

"Hannah and I think Searcy needed the Indian land the Echolses were squatting on to complete a large deer-hunt property to court potential clients for his private aircraft sales and service company in Oklahoma City—Buck Aviation. He must have done his land research at the Tish courthouse, too. Searcy needed realty leverage on the Echolses, who were squatting. And he found it in two men who were robbing pharmacies and stashing their take in a shack behind the Echols house—the one OSBI raided. The two men are Cleet Rankin, the Molotov guy in Johnston County lockup, and the redhead, Timothy . . ." He glanced at Magaw, bounced an index finger, and said, "Fletcher. I think the Echolses are addicted to Oxy, which Rankin and Fletcher supplied them in exchange for the stash shack. Probably how they got the shack in the first place."

Scrooby rolled the wadded paper ball back and forth between his hands on the spool table.

"How do you know . . ."

Maytubby was silent for a beat. "Let's just say I believe toxicology will bear me out."

Scrooby said nothing.

"Searcy could blackmail the Echolses," Maytubby said, "so that when Stan and Marva finally claimed the Indian land, they would sell it to him. We don't know exactly how Searcy first came to work with Rankin and Fletcher. But Hannah saw his Lincoln Navigator at their house on Chadwick Road outside Sulphur—and passing by Garn's garage in Tish."

Bond interrupted, "Nobody figgered on a Indian showin' up on Indian land. We think they lost their shit."

"Exactly," Maytubby said. "We think either the Echolses or Rankin or Fletcher caught Cy Mead scoping out his ancestor's land. Mead must have told one of them why he was there. That made him a threat on all sides. We don't know who killed Cy Mead, Agent Scrooby. Your ballistics lab and maybe your forensic anthropologist will help you determine that."

Scrooby drew himself up, swept his lunch trash off the table, folded his hands. "Go on," he said.

"Last night," Maytubby said, "I watched the Mead house in Cairo.

I knew the Echolses' lawyer, Fisk Bortel, had bonded them out. Searcy had the money to hire Bortel. I was worried that either the Echolses or Fletcher would threaten the surviving Meads. Or worse. Early this morning, the Echolses appeared in front of the Mead house on their motorcycle. I dissuaded them."

"*Dissuaded*," Scrooby said. He searched his attendants for humor and found none.

"Hannah?" Maytubby said.

"Back to where I left off," she said. "Red, Tim, Fletcher—whatever." She waved a hand above her head. "He decided he could get a bigger cut from the latest burglary—"

"She means," Maytubby said, "a pharmacy burglary in Kingston likely committed by Rankin and Fletcher after OSBI confiscated their Oxy at the Echols shack. I interviewed someone in Kingston who witnessed the Echolses drawing maps of the pharmacy."

Trooper Renaldo said, "Sergeant Maytubby alerted me to the possibility of a pharmacy burglary in my district, Troop F. He was correct. Kingston."

Hannah nodded. "A bigger cut if he joined up with these other maggots—Larry and Jerry. Red staged a holdup a little ways south of here so Larry and Jerry could make off with the new drugs and bring 'em to this shack. Bill and me had already trailed Larry and Jerry here after the fake holdup, which we witnessed. You got all the Oxy and all the guns we know about. Except LeeRoy's bazooka. I think Larry kept Princess's classy SIG pistol after the fake robbery. Used it to shoot my ear half off."

To Scrooby, Maytubby said, "We don't know about any firearms connected to the Echolses." He paused. "Do you?"

The shed fell silent.

"No comment," Scrooby said. He blew, then sat a moment. "We're done here. Sheriff Deane, I will contact you later this afternoon. Sergeant Maytubby and Deputy Bond, OSBI agents will interview you tomorrow in Sheriff Magaw's office in Tishomingo." He planted his knuckles on the spool table, heaved himself up, gathered the evidence sacks, and stalked out of the shed.

CHAPTER 34

Benny Magaw walked slowly to Bond and Maytubby and faced them. "Well done," he said. "Bill, I'll call Chief Fox right now and explain your work on this case. Maybe he'll cut you some slack on your summonses." He shook Maytubby's shoulder.

Maytubby said, "I took sick leave. Chief Fox might not take the news kindly."

"He's gonna find out anyway, Bill," Magaw said.

"True," Maytubby said.

Magaw turned to Bond. "Hannah, go home and heal. I'll put you down for three days of—"

"Bullshit," Hannah said.

Magaw laughed and walked out of the shed.

Maytubby and Bond walked along the rutted path, past the black GMC pickup. They struck the dirt road and followed it to Hannah's Skylark. "I ain't had no painkillers," she said. "I can drive fine."

CHAPTER 35

Maytubby drove up King's Road in Ada. His eyes smarted with fatigue. The low autumn sun didn't help. He shielded his eyes with his hand until he turned into Jill's driveway. He limped up the stairs to her garage apartment, let himself in, and fell on her couch.

A squeaking hinge in Jill's bedroom woke him. He sat up and swung his feet to the floor. His shoes were parked beside the couch. The windows were dark, and a dutch oven sat on the stove. He smelled cardamom and cumin. The Kitteridge novel was splayed on her kitchen table. "Jill?" he said.

She padded into the room in stocking feet. She wore jeans and an eggplant cable-knit sweater.

"Hey," she said. She knelt in front of him and laid her palms on his knees. "Your stomach was growling."

"What time is it?" he said.

"After ten," she said. "I ate earlier. Saved you some navy beans."

"Ten," he said. "At night?"

Jill smiled. "No. It's a solar eclipse. You should read the papers."

Maytubby stared at her, widened his eyes and shook his head. Then he smiled. "Cornbread?"

"Leftover corn tortillas."

"Even better," Maytubby said. He and Jill rose together. They embraced.

He winced as he limped to the stove. She rerouted him to the table, and he sat. "I got this, Sergeant," she said.

As she lit a kitchen match and fired up the burner under the beans, he said, "You and the stranger get all that food loaded in the mobile pantry truck?"

Jill stirred the beans with a wooden spoon. "Not only that, the stranger was a new nation hire, and he gave me a frozen wild tom he shot last week. It fit in my little freezer."

"Since you inhabit my déjà vu . . ."

"Ah, the deer hunter who gave me the sausage we cooked yesterday," Jill said.

"Was it yesterday, or centuries before?" Maytubby said.

Jill paused stirring. "That's your Emily Dickinson. Did you pick her up and put her back on your bedside table?"

"I did."

"The turkey guy worked hard, and he was no fun at all."

Maytubby laughed. "Then how'd you rate a tom?"

Jill thumped the wooden spoon on the lip of the dutch oven, turned off the burner, and rinsed the spoon in the sink. She took a ladle from the drawer, filled a bowl with beans, and set it on the table beside a soupspoon resting on a cloth napkin. "Ask me no questions, I'll tell you no lies," she said. She opened the oven, removed some foil-wrapped tortillas, and set them beside the bowl.

Maytubby ate with relish. Jill sat opposite him at the small dropleaf table. When he had finished the beans and tortillas, he carried his bowl and spoon to the sink, washed them and the spoon and ladle, and nestled them all in the dish drainer. He waved his hands to dry them and sat at the table.

"How is Hannah?" Jill said.

"She wouldn't take any painkillers when the doc sewed up her—"

"Helix."

"Right. She ate a few Slim Jims from her car when we got back to the crime scene—the shed west of Coalgate. After we told Scrooby what we had found, and laid out our theory of the plot, she said she could drive herself home," Maytubby said.

Jill picked up the splayed Kitteridge paperback, dog-eared her place, and set it on the table. "I take it Scrooby didn't welcome your fieldwork."

"He did not." Maytubby set his elbows on the table to ease the pain in his ribs. "But the truth let him save face. Only his forensic experts and labs can identify Cy Mead's killer."

"And did the truth make him puffed up?"

Maytubby laughed. "'Puffed up.' Our Sunday school days with the King James Bible strike home."

"Verily," Jill said.

Maytubby smiled. "He did puff up, but he cut us no slack. He stormed out of the shed."

"Are you and Hannah pissed because you didn't find the killer?"

"I can't speak for Hannah," Maytubby said. "But I am satisfied that the Meads will get justice."

"Yes," Jill said. She watched him. "You didn't say 'and claim their ancestor's allotment.' Because it would diminish Cy's death."

Maytubby nodded.

Jill was quiet for a beat. Then she said, "I think sitcom writers call this the MOS."

"The what?"

"The moment of shit. The abrupt sentimental turn."

"I see," Maytubby said. He continued, with mock gravity. "Olive Kitteridge wouldn't approve."

"Claptrap," Jill said in her Down East accent.

"Ayuh," Maytubby said.

Jill rose from the table and sat in his lap. "This will hurt your great toe," she said.

"Worth it."

"Olive wouldn't have called what you said claptrap," Jill said.

"I know," Maytubby said. He kissed Jill's neck. "She's blunt, but she's shrewd."

"Like Hannah."

"Yes," he said.

"Let's take a shower," Jill said.

"Hot biscuits!" Maytubby said.

"And then look after that great toe."

As she unbuttoned his shirt, Maytubby said, "You've told me hotter things."

CHAPTER 36

A week later, in the early afternoon, Maytubby drove Hannah to the Mead house in Cairo. The bandage on her ear was smaller than the one from the ER. He parked his Ford in the driveway, next to his aunt Lydia's old Honda.

The white chow, Blanche, jogged to the pickup, her tail wagging. Maytubby got out and petted her. Rose Turner held the front door open for Maytubby, Hannah, and Blanche. As Hannah walked in, Rose said, "Oh, Lord, your poor ear. Bill told me."

Hannah nodded quickly and did not stop.

Maytubby's aunt and Linda Mead, Cy's mother, sat at a round oak table. Green Fire-King mugs sat in front of them—one in front of Rose Turner's empty chair. There were three half-eaten slices of pecan pie on saucers beside the mugs. Linda Mead had dark circles under her eyes. She had lost weight. Maytubby's aunt sat very close to her and occasionally patted her back.

After salutations, Rose brought Hannah and Maytubby coffee and pie. Then she sat in her chair, next to Maytubby, and took a sip of coffee. She nodded toward Maytubby. "Thank you, Sergeant."

Simultaneously, Maytubby said, "Bill" and his aunt said, "William."

"William," Rose said, "and . . ."

"Deputy Hannah," Aunt Lydia said.

"Deputy Hannah," Rose said, nodding toward her, "for coming this afternoon." Cy's mother and Aunt Lydia nodded solemnly. "We know the state investigators have not yet found Cy's killer. But we are grateful, William, that you called Linda when Cy's, uh, remains were identified with dental records. The truth was ugly, but you told it straight." Rose paused. "Before some government stranger could pretty it up."

"Thank you, Rose," Maytubby said.

"We know," she said, "you and Deputy Hannah have risked your lives to see justice done for Cy."

Hannah nodded. When Rose sank her fork into the remains of her pie, Hannah followed suit, and so did Maytubby. Forks clinked on saucers. The white chow, lying on the floor, her head between her paws, sighed with a vague whimper.

"*Ofi' Tobhi*," Maytubby said.

Aunt Lydia beamed. "You remember that, William." She turned in her chair and looked down at Blanche. Then she chuckled. "I'm afraid *that* white dog's path leads to her food bowl."

Maytubby smiled. The others looked stumped.

When Rose and Maytubby had carried the saucers and forks to the kitchen and taken their seats again, Maytubby said, "Please let me know when Cy's funeral will be held. Johnson Chapel?"

Rose said, "Yes."

Maytubby looked around the table. "Is it too soon to bring up Augustus Mead's allotment?"

Rose did not consult the table. "No," she said. "Cy sacrificed his life to bring it back into his family."

Maytubby watched Linda Mead, who nodded vigorously and pointed a quaking index finger at him. She began to cry and pinched her nose. Aunt Lydia put her arm around her.

Maytubby took a card from his shirt pocket, laid it on the table, and slid it to Rose. He said, "The squatters on Augustus Mead's land, Stan and Marva Echols, have been put back into the Johnston County jail.

Their bond was revoked by a county judge after they appeared at this house to threaten your family. They will forfeit their claim to the land. Just in the nick of time, too. They were a month shy of living there for fifteen years."

Hannah said, "That's how long squatters have to stay before they take over."

Maytubby nodded. "Hannah's land expert friend did all the research. She discovered Augustus's patent. But Cy had done that long before she did."

Rose picked up the card and read it. "Go on," she said.

Maytubby turned to her. "That's a title attorney I know in Ada. She's Chickasaw. I've told her about your case, and she wants to help you reclaim the allotment. Your family is, of course, free to choose another attorney."

"*Yakoke*," Lydia said. Thank you.

Maytubby said, "I will call Linda as soon as I learn the results of the state investigators' work." He and Hannah rose. "Thank you all for the coffee and pie," he said. "I am so sorry for your terrible loss. Cy was a caring young man who looked after his people."

"Yes, he was." Rose stood. "And he did."

CHAPTER 37

A week before Christmas, Maytubby and Jill, Hannah and LeeRoy Sickles, Rose Turner, Sheriff Magaw, Lighthorse Chief Fox, and "Garn" Garner seated themselves at a long rustic table at Stingley's BBQ in south Ada. The room was cavernous and dark, paneled with knotty pine. Mounted buck heads stared from the walls. In one corner, a small artificial Christmas tree sat atop a stool. Its tiny lights blinked feebly.

Hannah no longer wore a bandage. The top of her left ear bore a jagged notch. She was in uniform. Sheriff Magaw had granted her two hours' leave from her shift in Johnston County.

Before a waitress appeared, Hannah said, "Where is Agent Scrooby?" She turned to Maytubby. "You invited him. Right, Bill?"

Everyone laughed but Rose Turner, who looked around quizzically.

Maytubby said to Rose, "He's a state cop nobody likes."

Rose nodded and smiled.

"But," Maytubby said, "he helped us solve this case."

LeeRoy, who wore denim overalls and a red button-down shirt crowned with a silver-tipped bolo tie, said, "He the feller sent that damn kid to my house to ask me fool questions?" LeeRoy probed the top pockets of his overalls for a cigarette.

"You can't smoke in here," Hannah said.

He let his hands fall on the table.

"Yes," Maytubby said.

LeeRoy welcomed the news. "That hopper stuck a thing in my mouth. To get my DNA, he said, 'cause I left cigarette butts at *the scene*. He also tried to take my boots. For evidence! I told him to go to hell, that's the only shoes I got. So, tell me. Did that redhead peckerwood take some o' my bird shot?"

Hannah turned to him, "You know he did. I already told you that."

LeeRoy smiled and juked his head. "You're ruinin' my story, Hannah."

The waitress setting out their waters frowned and side-eyed the table.

Maytubby introduced Rose to the company while they received their plastic menus.

Hannah glanced at her menu and tossed it on the table. "Rose makes the best pecan pie," she said.

Everyone looked at Rose Turner. "*Yakoke*," she said to Hannah.

"Is that Indian-speak?" LeeRoy said.

Rose said to him, "Yes, it is. Deputy Hannah is learning Chickasaw."

LeeRoy gaped. "*Han*nah."

"Hush," Hannah said.

When the waitress returned, Maytubby and Jill ordered dinner salads. Hannah looked at them and said, "I know you two eat real food when nobody's lookin'." She turned to LeeRoy and said, "Bill's buyin'. I'm goin' the whole hog. Rib dinner. You should, too. You're so skinny, people start callin' you Slats."

"Hee hee hee," LeeRoy convulsed, then dug for cigarettes.

Maytubby was off duty. He wore a maroon button-down shirt and jeans. Jill, on her lunch break from the Chickasaw Nation, wore a navy skirt suit and compulsory pantyhose. After everyone had ordered lunch, Maytubby looked around the table and said, "Some of you know all the results of the Cy Mead murder investigation.

Others know pieces. So Hannah and I will tell the tale quick as we can, before we eat. Hannah?"

She cleared her throat and looked above the heads of those seated at the table. "Well. My landman-woman friend Patty went down to the courthouse in Tish and found out about the Indian Mead land thing," she twirled her hand in the air, "and about that bigwig—Searcy—owning all the land around it. Bill and me figured he was puttin' together deer land for his, uh, business crap. Turns out he was." Hannah laid her hands palm down on the table. "Go on, Bill."

"Mitchell Searcy spilled the beans to Scrooby in a plea bargain. Four years ago, Searcy went to the courthouse in Tish and discovered the Mead patent. He went to the land and confronted the Echolses, who were squatting on it. He told them what he knew and offered to buy them a house and acreage north of Ten-Acre Rock if they completed their adverse possession claim and then sold the Mead land to him. The Echolses balked. Searcy dug around and found out they were opioid addicts—Stan from an old injury, and Marva from living with Stan. Searcy learned that they traded with their pushers for the use of the shed behind their house as a stash. The opioid burglars and runners were Timothy Fletcher—the redhead—"

"Oooooh, goddamn," LeeRoy purred. His hands did the marionette dance above the table. Fox and Magaw smiled. Hannah did not.

"—and Cleet Rankin," Maytubby said.

"Princess," Hannah said. Dishes clattered in the kitchen. Pecan smoke from the barbecue pit drifted into the room.

"Yes," Maytubby said. "Searcy struck blackmail gold in Fletcher and Rankin and put them on his payroll. The Echolses were beaten. They agreed to sell him their stolen land.

"One day, Cy Mead"—he nodded somberly at Rose—"Rose Turner's grandson, appeared on the squatters' land, his ancestor's land, and innocently told the Echolses why he was there. They told Fletcher, Rankin, and Searcy. The Echolses were so near closing on the land, everybody panicked. Fletcher and Rankin took matters into their own hands, forced Cy Mead's car off the road at Rock Creek, killed him, and burned his body in the Echolses' charcoal kiln."

"I found that mess when I was huntin' squirrels." LeeRoy shook his head sadly.

Sheriff Magaw said, "Thank you, Mr. Sickles. We are in your debt."

LeeRoy jerked his head up and jiggled his black-rimmed glasses. "You don't owe me nothin'. Hannah fried up them squirrels. They was good eatin'."

Hannah did a fair imitation of Scrooby's pissed blow.

Maytubby paused. Then he said, "The Echolses scouted the pharmacy marks for Fletcher and Rankin. At some point, Tim Fletcher decided he could sweeten his cut if he ditched his partner and teamed up with the crooked twins Larry and Jerry O'Hara. He staged a hijack west of Coalgate so the twins could make off with the latest score, from a pharmacy in Kingston."

"We saw that go down," Hannah said. "Larry tossed a pistol they stole in the fake robbery out their muscle-car window. Me and Bill went back and found it in a sumac stand."

"Hannah brought it to me," Magaw said, "and I turned it over to Scrooby."

Maytubby nodded. "The Oklahoma medical examiner's forensic anthropologist identified Cy's body with dental records from a Coalgate dentist. The State Bureau's DNA expert found two traces of DNA on the pistol—Larry O'Hara's and Tim Fletcher's. Since Larry had thrown out the pistol after the hijacking, the gun belonged to Fletcher—Red. OSBI recovered two bullets from Cy's abandoned Ford Focus. One of them, in the passenger headrest, was intact. And it was fired from Fletcher's pistol."

"The shit-for-brains," Hannah mumbled.

"The pistol Larry *didn't* toss out, the one they stole from Cleet Rankin—"

"That's the fancy SIG that Larry tried to kill me with," Hannah said. She pointed to the notch on her ear. "You see, that's all he done. He was better at shootin' dope the maggots sold him."

"Fletcher has been charged with first-degree murder. Because the US Supreme Court recently restored the old boundaries of the Chickasaw Nation, the US Attorney for Eastern Oklahoma is prosecuting the murder. The other actors have been charged by tribal and state governments with accessory to murder, conspiracy, attempted murder, and burglary." Maytubby surveyed the downcast faces around the table. He said, "These are grim tidings, for the season. But we will soon receive more comforting news, from Rose, about the Mead family."

Maytubby took his glass of ice water in hand but left it on the table. "Stingley's doesn't have a liquor license, but let's have a toast to Garn. His quick thinking and bravery preserved vital evidence in this case."

Garn sat in the shadows at the far end of the table. He had donned fresh coveralls and combed his thinning hair.

Maytubby stood and raised his glass. The rest of the table stood—all but Garn. Sheriff Magaw, next to him, pulled him up gently by his armpit and said, "This is for you, Garn."

"What?" Garn said.

"To Garn!" Maytubby said.

"To Garn!" the table echoed. They clinked water glasses.

Garn stared around the table, astonished, and then sank into his chair. Sheriff Magaw laid his right hand on Garn's back.

Everyone sat. Maytubby was silent for a minute.

Rose spoke up. "Bill—William—has good manners. He knows this talk of Cy's killing pains me. But I'm tough." She nodded toward Bond. "Like Deputy Hannah." LeeRoy giggled. "Thanks to everyone here, justice has been done. Bill gave me and my daughter Linda— Cy's mother—the name of a title attorney. We contacted her. Our family has reclaimed Augustus Mead's allotment."

There were nods and murmurs around the table.

"Linda is having the old house plumbed and wired by friends in Cairo and Coalgate. She plans to move there in the spring."

"I didn't know that, Rose." Maytubby put his arm around Jill. "We're happy for you."

"Thank you," Rose said. She paused and then said softly to

Maytubby, "And if you're wondering, Blanche stays with me." She smiled mischievously.

The waitress began delivering plates. Tishomingo country music star Blake Shelton's "You Make It Feel like Christmas" wafted in from the kitchen.

As Hannah watched the waitress's hands for her rib dinner, she said, "That song's corny."

CHAPTER 38

Maytubby and Jill said goodbye to all their guests. Maytubby paid the tab. They pulled on their coats and stepped out of the restaurant. The first snow of the year drifted from a scudding cloud bank. Heavy flakes landed on their hair.

They kissed and held each other.

When they stepped back, still holding hands, Maytubby said, "Is this the 'moment of shit' you speak of?"

Jill smiled. "You bet your sweet ass it is."

ACKNOWLEDGMENTS

A shout-out to my wife, Karleene Smith, who is a tough reader.

My editor, Michael Carr, is God's gift—and a fellow southern plainsman who knows the territory.

I owe much to these wonderful folks for their professional advice: tribal nutritionists Sarah Miracle and Jill Fox, pharmacist Karen Tobey, Drs. Michael and Myrna Pontious, Detective Robert Kelson, title attorney Rick Poland, ballistics expert Jerry Carter, Physician Assistant Natalie Campbell, OME forensic anthropologist Angela Berg, OSBI DNA specialist Rhonda Williams, and scoreboard technicians Rick and Fannie Davis. Any mistakes on these counts are down to me.

Deep thanks to keen readers and critics: Désirée Hupy, Joel Morgan, Joan Schoenfeld, Chris Suit, Karie Camp, and Olivier Bourderionnet.

I am indebted to Ben Hutchens for his knowledge of casino security and to Sam Higgins, who manages my website.

Thanks to Chickasaw citizens Darlene Brown and Mary Colburn for their help with scenes involving customs unfamiliar to me.

The Chickasaw Lighthorse Police Department has answered all my queries politely and promptly.

Jason Eyechabbe taught me what little Chickasaw I know. He edited the Chickasaw passages in this novel. Former Chickasaw Lighthorse chief of police Jason O'Neill patiently explained the intricacies of tribal jurisdiction. Since our interview some years ago, the US Supreme Court's McGirt decision has ceded more power to tribal and federal law enforcement in Oklahoma's Indian Country.

I am indebted to historian John P. Dyson, author of *The Early Chickasaw Homeland*, for information about tribal contact with John Wesley.

Deep thanks to the bakers and baristas at Gray Owl Coffee Shop, in Norman, Oklahoma, where I write every day: Jenny, Laura, Chris, Braden, Roshni, Erica, Emily, Anastasia, Katie, and Isaac.

A salute to the book designers, Zena Coffman, Djamika Smith, Sean Thomas, Amy Craig, and Alex Cruz. And to Mark Bramhall, soulful audio voice of the series.

Kudos to my sedulous line editor, Ember Hood.

And, finally, a toast to my agent Richard Curtis and to Blackstone publicists Lauren Maturo and Isabella Nugent, who carry Maytubby and Bond into the wide, wide world.